HARDLY WORKING

HARDLY WORKING

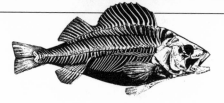

STORIES BY

RICHARD THORMAN

Louisiana State University Press

Baton Rouge and London 1990

First printing

99 98 97 96 95 94 93 92 91 90   5 4 3 2 1

Designer: Laura Roubique Gleason
Typeface: ITC Galliard
Typesetter: The Composing Room of Michigan, Inc.
Printer and Binder: Thomson-Shore, Inc.

LIBRARY OF CONGRESS CATALOGING-IN-PUBLICATION DATA

Thorman, Richard.
  Hardly working : stories / by Richard Thorman.
      p.   cm.
  ISBN 0-8071-1583-5 (alk. paper)
  I. Title.
PS3570.H6479H3   1990
813'.54—dc20   89-34631
                                                              CIP

This publication was made possible in part by grants from the Maryland
State Arts Council and the National Endowment for the Arts.

"The Box of Contents" was originally published in *The Virginia Quarterly
Review,* LXI (Summer, 1985), 433–52; "Hardly Working" first appeared in
The Sewanee Review, XCIII:4 (Fall, 1985), 507–25; "The Family Man" was
first published in *The Sewanee Review,* XCV:3 (Summer, 1987), 369–87;
"The Hired Man" originally appeared in *The Long Story,* No. 5 (Spring,
1987), 22–41; and "The Stradivarius" was first published in *The Southern
Review,* n.s., XX:2 (April, 1984), 387–405.

The paper in this book meets the guidelines for permanence and durability
of the Committee on Production Guidelines for Book Longevity of the
Council on Library Resources. ∞

This book is for George Core

CONTENTS

The Box of Contents   1

Hardly Working   21

The Heart of Donald Duck   40

The Family Man   59

The Hired Man   78

The Stradivarius   106

HARDLY WORKING

THE BOX OF CONTENTS

It was going to be a burner, one of those days when you wake up and the soles of your feet are wet with sweat. The way it had been, one day after another, with no letup. After a while it gets to a man, unhinges his brain, assuming he had some sense to start with. That's what happened to Billy Floyd at the auction sale. The heat wasn't the only reason, but folks understand weather. The sun shines on the sinners and the saved.

In Billy's case the reason he acted the way he did was in his blood and the heat just brought it out. For as far back as anyone knew Billy's people had never amounted to squat. Lots of high-flown notions and plenty of excuses. There was something downright childish about all of them but without the innocence folks are always hanging on children. I never held with that idea anyway. Some people go to the grave without learning anything. You can call that innocence if you've a mind, but to me it's plain dumb.

People looked out for the Floyds because God knows they couldn't fend for themselves, brought them food out of the garden or invented jobs for Billy. Each time Billy would stick his hands in the bib of his overalls, grin, and say, "You didn't have to do that." Hell, we knew we didn't have to, but if we didn't who would?

There's nothing new about auction sales. The minute a man had something to sell there was someone around to sell it for him and someone else to buy it as long as it was cheap enough. That's human nature. And there never was a shortage of reasons for a sale. Sometimes it's a case of a man selling out because he's tired, or sick, or sick and tired. Or maybe he drops dead, like Henry Sterret did, and his widow lets herself get talked into selling everything she and Henry put together, plus all the things that were handed down from generation to generation and haven't been out of the family for one hundred fifty years and more, so she can buy a condominium in Florida, or some damned place.

The hottest day of the year was exactly the sort of day Beulah Sterret would pick to hold her sale. I went to school with Beulah and thought for a while I might marry her, but Henry came along and saved me. As she grew older Beulah got the habit of saying "what" to anything. She claimed she was hard of hearing, but it was just her way. You had to say things twice, sometimes three times before you could get an answer from her. The wife maintains it's hard enough to get me to say things once.

Having what you might call a family interest, there was no way I was going to miss this sale. If I went for no other reason, I was determined that Beulah get enough money, as long as it wasn't mine. The wife had her eye on Beulah's pie safe. I couldn't see that it was much different from ours, but I learned long ago not to argue about things like that.

I could see right away that this was going to be the biggest sale of the year. We arrived at the Sterret place in plenty of time, but it was all I could do to fit the pickup into the pasture that had been turned into a parking lot. There were maybe twenty people in line to sign up and get their number. Not just the usual folks, but people who had come out from town, plus antique dealers. You can tell the dealers by the way they dress. Local folks put on clean clothes to go to a sale. Dealers don't care what they wear.

I was glad to see Ferris Bull would be the auctioneer. Not everybody would agree, of course, because if you put it to a vote ten percent of the people would hold that the world is flat, but it's pretty generally accepted that Ferris is the best.

He was thanking the crowd for showing up—he always starts that way, then thanks them again during the sale and at the end—because people like to feel good about themselves. "Can you hear me back there?" he yelled. Then he made some jokes about the heat. Nothing funny, just to get folks in the proper frame of mind. He introduced his wife, who sat under a beach umbrella at a little table behind him and wrote down the number of each buyer and what he bid, so when it came time to settle up, there could be no argument. Then he introduced his two assistants, who held up what he was selling so everybody could see what they were bidding on. Finally he gave the rules, which weren't all that complicated: if you were top bidder, you bought it, had to pay for it, and have it off the property by the end of the day.

The thing about Ferris is that he'll stop right in the middle of the bidding to kid along with the folks. If someone drops out he'll say something like, "We had a good time while it lasted, didn't we?" Or if a lady can't make up her mind whether she wants in or out he'll say, "Don't worry, ma'am, you haven't spent it yet." But the thing I like best is that he works just as hard over a box of contents as for a bush hog. He'll squeeze out the last quarter like if he didn't get it he, the widow he's selling for, the county, the state, and maybe the whole damned country was heading for the poorhouse. I admire that in a man.

I'll explain a box of contents because it has to do with Billy Floyd and what happened. A box of contents is just like it says, a collection of junk that isn't worth the effort to throw away but represents the principle that there is nothing in this world someone won't buy if you put it together with more of the same and the price is low enough.

I hadn't taken two steps before Billy Floyd, Box of Contents Billy, saw me. He was standing to one side, getting what shade he could from a catalpa. On either side of him were his boys, looking so much like their father it was as if they had no mother at all. The same round face, pale kinky hair sticking out the side of CAT caps, red-rimmed eyes like they were coming down with sties. They even stood with their hands tucked into the bibs of their overalls.

Ferris sang his first "Lookee here," which is the way he introduces each object before trying for an opening bid.

"It's a burner," Billy said.

"You can say that again." There's no need to try and say something smart about the weather.

"Good crowd."

"Sure is."

I turned and saw Ferris take off his cowboy hat, wipe his forehead with the end of a towel his wife kept for him, then begin his song. Any auctioneer worth anything has some phrase he sings over and over. It doesn't have to make sense because all it does is keep the sound going between the numbers. Ferris's is, "What'll ye give?"

"I want you to meet my boys," Billy said. "This here is Bobby. And this is Rich."

I shook hands with them. Ferris was on the money now and singing away. "How's your wife?" I asked.

"Compared to what?" He laughed so hard people turned around to see what was funny. "She got a cold. Ain't that something, a cold in this heat?"

I started to edge away. "Got to find the wife."

"She's over there." He nodded and kept his hands in his bib. You had to think that maybe his chest would fall off if he didn't keep hold of it. "Talking to Missus Sterret."

Ferris was on his next "Lookee here," working his way through a table of dishes and pots.

I found the wife sitting beside Beulah, both of them working up a sweat fanning themselves.

"You want to give Ferris that fan," I said. "I bet it would fetch a good price on a day like this."

Beulah smiled at me and said, "What?"

"He says you could sell your fan," the wife said.

"Why would I want to do that?" Beulah asked. She was wearing a straw hat, fastened under her chin with a pull string. It covered her white hair without hiding it. Didn't hide her dark blue eyes either. If anything, it made them bluer than ever. Her eyes were always her best feature.

"Good crowd," I said.

The wife jumped right in before Beulah could "What?" me. "He says there's a lot of people."

4

Beulah smiled. Either the dentist did one hell of a job or those were still her teeth. Her smile was another of her good features. "Henry and I have a lot of friends. I hope I'm doing what he would have wanted, selling out and moving to Florida."

"Of course you are, dear," the wife said.

"You think so?"

I wondered how Beulah could hear the wife but need an interpreter for me.

"I keep thinking," Beulah said, then stopped as if she forgot what she was thinking. "When I move away I won't be able to be with Henry."

If you want to be with him all you have to do is take up residence in the cemetery, which I don't see you being in such an all-fired hurry to do.

I didn't say it, but the wife looked at me as if I had.

"Billy Floyd came over to pay his respects," Beulah said. "Of course Henry was always good to him."

"Henry was good to everyone," the wife said.

"Had his boys with him," Beulah went on as though she hadn't heard the wife. "The three of them like peas in a pod."

The fact is Henry Sterret was better than good to Billy. All of us did our share of looking out for the Floyds, but Henry worked it overtime. If all Billy paid was respects in exchange for all the hard money Henry paid him, then Billy was miles ahead.

"I'll see you later, Beulah," I said.

And naturally she answered, "What?"

Ferris had cleared the first table and was working on a box of contents. Of course Billy was right up front, raising the bid from a quarter to fifty cents. Four bits was about his limit, but he was known to go as high as a dollar. Above seventy-five cents he moved ten cents at a time. Would have moved at a nickel pace if Ferris had let him.

The wife found me standing in front of the barn, looking over the tools that would be put up for sale.

"I guessed I'd find you here," she said.

"You guessed right."

"Don't tell me there's a tool in this world you don't already own."

She said not to tell her, so that's what I did. But you don't get the better of that woman so easy.

"Looks like old junk to me."

"Mostly is. Appears she already sold anything worth owning. At least I hope she did and didn't give it to the son-in-law."

"That reminds me."

It didn't remind her. Almost nothing I say ever does.

"Reminds you of what?" I couldn't resist.

"I talked to Beulah. She wants us to have the pie safe, so she's going to tell Ferris to hold it back near the end. That way some of those dealers may give up and go home before the bidding."

"She wants us to have it she could give it to us." I didn't say a word about "us" wanting the pie safe.

"I thought I'd tell you, so you don't go wandering off. I want you with me when Ferris puts it up."

What she wanted was an accomplice. She was bound and determined to get that pie safe and wanted me standing next to her so when she bid more than the damned thing was worth I couldn't come back at her later for spending too much.

"That cultivator looks interesting," she said.

"The colter is missing."

"Never mind. I bet one of those dealers will be glad to get it." All the time she was talking she was stirring the air with her straw fan, not cooling anything but spreading the heat more evenly. "You look hot," she said. "The ladies from the rescue squad auxiliary are selling ice tea behind the house."

"You want some?"

"That would be nice. And see if they have any crumb cake."

"Where will you be?"

"Right here."

I must have stood in line thirty minutes. Somebody I never saw spilled Coca-Cola on my fresh shirt, then when I finally got the ice tea and crumb cake a woman backed into me and dropped tea all down the front of my pants. Of course the wife wasn't where she said she'd be.

I found her sitting with Mrs. Ramsey, who took one look at me, pointed to my pants, and laughed.

"Looks like you had yourself an accident," she said.

I told her the accident wasn't all mine and gave her my ice tea.

I heard Ferris announce that as soon as he finished selling what he was on he was going to move down to the barn and sell the tools, so that's where I headed.

There was no breeze, not even a whisper. If you so much as shuffled your feet a cloud of red dust rose maybe six inches off the ground and hung there. A soul fresh from hell would feel right at home, might even ask for a cold drink to cool down. A few at a time, folks began to gather. The red dust was thicker and rose higher. It was a different crowd from the one that had been bidding near the house. There were more farmers, fewer women, not so many young people, and just a sprinkling of damned dealers with their shirts open clean down to their waists and dirty-looking handkerchiefs knotted around their necks. There was a fat one with pants drooping low on his hips who looked like a candidate for heat stroke. His hair was strung down his neck and he kept shaking his head as if he couldn't believe what was happening to him. With every step he planted his foot like he was coming down stairs and wasn't sure where the last step was.

The tea had dried on my pants, leaving a ring and a rusty stain. I edged over to stand next to Fatso because no matter how grubby I looked I had to be better than him.

"I never knew it could get this hot," he said.

"It's a burner," I allowed.

Ferris was bent almost double to hang onto the sidewall of his pickup as one of his assistants drove it down the grade to the barn. His shirt was wet clean across the back and under the arms, and there was a wet spot in the center of his chest. "We're going to sell all the tools," he announced, "and then we'll sell the wagon."

All the time I had been standing there I had seen only the burned-out motors, the pumps and wrenches, the mauls and axes with busted helves, the horse collars and hames, and I hadn't even noticed the wagon. A wagon is not something a man is likely to overlook. I moved forward as if it was a mirage and I had to touch it to be sure it was real.

It appeared to be some twelve feet long, flat bed with almost new two-inch boards over a steel frame. You could use it to haul all kind of heavy equipment. At the back was a pair of hinged ramps that folded onto the bed, and there were U-bolts front and rear to chain down whatever it was you were carrying. Henry must have rigged it out himself. He was always good at things like that. There were rubber tires and the frame had been lengthened. You could put two small tractors on it and have room to spare. I knew I didn't have to check the hitch, not if it was put on by Henry Sterret, but I did anyway.

Ferris had given I don't know how many "Lookee here's" and was singing away by the time I got through looking the wagon over. Now, I'm not saying I needed it, but I never met a farmer who had too many wagons, any more than I met a woman who had too many clothes, or didn't need another pie safe. I didn't mean to chase it out of sight, but as long as the price was right I wouldn't mind owning it. I looked around to see who might bid against me. Near as I could tell there were four. I knew Sam Baldwin and Mike Browner. Neither of them would bid high. The other two I never saw before.

"Nice-looking wagon," someone said.

I looked up and there was Billy Floyd grinning across from me. His boys were still beside him, each with a box of contents tucked under an arm. I looked away from them and checked my watch like I was worried about the time. It would make no sense to praise something I was thinking about bidding on.

I moved back beside the fat man, who had bid in the cultivator with the missing colter, and I never would find out what it brought. He was bidding on an old grain shovel with a crack in the handle. The bid was one hundred dollars and damned if he didn't raise it. I moved away from him in case whatever he had was contagious.

As the red dust rose so did the prices. I figured if I ever emptied out my barn I could be a damned millionaire.

When the last rusty rake and burned-out motor was sold Ferris mopped his face. Word of the prices must have spread and folks wanted to see who was spending the money. All the people who had been waiting up at the house for the furniture and clocks to go moved down to the barn. The dust was almost as high as the wagon bed and so thick people were fanning it away, which only made it worse.

Any auctioneer likes for there to be a lot of people, but Ferris had to know that there wasn't more than a handful of us who were ready to bid. Maybe he thought he could get some excitement going or at least have some fun. He gave a "Lookee here," then stepped onto the tailgate of his pickup and half jumped to the wagon. He stomped his heel on the boards to show how solid it was.

"How thick you reckon these boards are?" he asked me.

"Inch," I lied.

"Two," Mike Browner said.

"More like three I'd guess," Ferris smiled. He pranced up and down the wagon, pointing out features like he knew what he was talking about. "All right, folks," he yelled. "What we got us here is an A-number-one flat-bed wagon. It was Henry Sterret's and he wouldn't have had it unless it was the best. What am I bid? Who'll start at four hundred just to get on the money?"

The wagon was worth all that and more, but wouldn't nobody in his right mind start there. I was willing for the bidding to end there and maybe go some higher, but if that's where you began there would be no telling where it would go.

Nobody said a word at four, so Ferris right away dropped to three and sort of leaned back on his heels like he was doing everyone a favor to start so low. Still no one said anything. "Two hundred and let's go," Ferris barked, making believe he was disgusted with us for being cheapskates.

"Fifty," Billy Floyd said.

"Thank you, Billy," Ferris smiled. Then he stopped, pushed his hat back, and puckered his lips. "Billy ever tell you about the time this stranger come up and asked him, 'You lived here all your life?' Know what Billy told him?" Everybody knew what was coming, so Ferris waited while we got ready to laugh. "'Not yet,'" he finally said.

To me that's a funny story and I laugh every time I hear it. But Billy practically doubled over laughing. In the end folks were laughing at him more than at Ferris's story. Maybe that's where things began to get out of hand.

"All right," Ferris said, then had to say it three or four more times before folks settled down. "We're on the money at fifty dollars. Do I hear one hundred?" And he started singing.

If he was going to get fifty-dollar jumps it wouldn't be any time before he was back where he wanted to begin. "Not so fast, Ferris," I complained. "We got plenty of time."

Ferris changed his tune to seventy-five and Sam Baldwin got in. Ferris was asking one hundred now and got it right off from one of the two men I didn't know but who I figured would bid. I hung back because it doesn't matter who has the first bid, it's who has the last one that counts.

The bidding was getting close to three hundred and I was ready to begin. Ferris was singing away and waving his arms. Then for no reason I could figure out, except that he liked the attention his first bid brought him, Billy Floyd loosened one hand from the bib of his overalls and put in a bid of three twenty-five, skipping right past three hundred.

Billy Floyd bidding three hundred and twenty-five dollars made less sense than the fat dealer bidding more than one hundred for a busted grain shovel. At least the dealer figured he could sell the damned thing for more than he paid. Come to think of it, that may have been Billy's idea too, but no one will ever convince me that Billy had any idea what the wagon was really worth. He had no experience and even if he had, the Floyds were the sort of people who don't profit from mistakes but go on making them as long as they live. I'm not saying he didn't have the money, or couldn't borrow it, because he was always a hard worker and had a good name for paying what he owed, but he needed that wagon like a bull needs teats, or Ferris Bull needs another mouth.

In any case, Ferris shouldn't have done what he did next, not with Billy's boys standing beside him. He turned away so Billy couldn't see him and winked at the crowd, and them damned fools smiled back and encouraged him.

Ferris started singing for three fifty and got it without trying too hard. Then he turned back to Billy and asked for three seventy-five. Billy grinned at him and nodded.

Four hundred came and went. Then four fifty. And it was Billy bidding against the field. As soon as it got over five fifty, even those who hadn't seen Ferris wink knew what was going on. Maybe Billy knew it too, but there was no way for him to back off, not with his boys standing beside him.

The bid was running up to seven hundred and folks were starting to laugh. Not just those who knew Billy and knew that he lived in a tenant house that didn't have even a nodding acquaintance with paint, where a flush toilet was still a sort of novelty, but even the town folks and the dealers. It was all in fun, though I didn't think it was funny. And there was Billy, his face red and sweating, his red-rimmed eyes bulging. He knew folks were laughing at him, and of course it made him dig in his heels. I felt so sorry for the damned fool, but I didn't see how I could make him stop.

Everybody was joining in the bidding now because they knew no matter what they bid, Billy would bid more. When it got to a thousand dollars the laughter was so loud Ferris could barely hear the bid. At eleven hundred everybody broke off at the same time. Fun is fun, they must have figured, but it was getting so high they were afraid Billy might stop too.

Billy still grinned but there was a look of terror in his eyes. If a hole had opened in the ground, he would gladly have dropped through it and just kept going. He stuck his hand back in his bib and looked around for someone, anyone, to continue bidding. Maybe he didn't know what the wagon was worth, but he had to know that at eleven hundred dollars he was the sort of fool people would talk about forever. "Remember the day Billy Floyd bid eleven hundred for that wagon?" And everybody who heard would start laughing.

Ferris closed out the bidding fast and Billy's hand shook as he raised the pasteboard with his number on it. The wagon was his. It might take him a year of paying interest to pay for it, and during that time maybe his family wouldn't eat so good, or the kids get new clothes, and all of us would have to invent more jobs than ever for him, but he owned a flat-bed wagon that wasn't good for anything except carrying heavy equipment that he didn't own and never would.

Folks were buzzing and had stopped laughing. Ferris sensed the change in mood. It was all fun as long as the bidding went on, but now that it was done and they could see the panic on Billy's face the fun was over. Ferris runs an honest sale, as honest as an auction sale can be, and if anything is misrepresented, even by accident, the buyer has the option of refusing purchase and it goes up for bids again. Those are the rules.

"Now, if this wagon ain't exactly what we said it was—" Ferris began.

"The hitch is busted," I snapped back.

"Man says the hitch is busted," Ferris yelled into the microphone. There was a kind of sigh from the crowd. "Take a look at it, Billy," Ferris said.

It was his way out. I don't care how dumb he was, he had to know it. All he had to do was look at the hitch and nod his head, not even say a word, just nod. Nobody would say a thing about there being nothing wrong with the hitch, and the bidding would start over again.

Sweat rolled down Billy's neck, soaking his shirt and leaking clean through his overalls. He walked all around the wagon before he reached the hitch. Bent over to examine it, then kicked it once from each side.

"Ain't nothing wrong with it," he said. He had to swallow in the middle to get the last words out. The minute he said it something happened to me. I still felt sorry for him, but I was mad because he didn't seem to give a damn what I felt.

"You sure?" Ferris asked.

Billy stood straight, his face wet, his hands stuck back in his bib. "I'm sure."

Ferris looked at me, then looked at the crowd and shrugged.

"All right, folks," he said, "we're going to move back up to the house now and sell the furniture. If anyone needs some refreshment, the ladies from the rescue squad auxiliary have a stand over there."

The crowd moved off, following Ferris in the pickup and raising a fresh cloud of dust. Billy stood beside his wagon—it was sure as hell his now. His eyes bugged, sweat rolled off his face like it was tears, his mouth opened but still with that damned grin. His arms hung at his sides and you could see the fiery scar on the inside of his left forearm where he pinched it in a baler. His boys were still beside him, each clutching his box of contents.

It didn't seem right to leave him there, but it wasn't right to go on staring at him like he was a prize fool, which of course he was. I started to ease away and was almost to the incline leading back to the house before Billy caught me.

"That's a fine wagon," he said.

I allowed as there was nothing wrong with the wagon.

"Man could haul a lot of equipment on a wagon like that."

I allowed that too.

"Saw you looking at it," Billy said. "Thought maybe you were going to bid."

"I considered it."

"Fact is—" Billy stuck his hands back in his bib, which made him look more natural, and ducked in front of me like he was afraid I might run off. "Fact is, you could use a wagon like that."

"A man can always use a good wagon."

"I could let you have it for fifty dollars over what I paid."

"I don't think so, Billy."

He blinked a couple of times to get the sweat out of his eyes. "Look, you always been fair with me. I'll let you have it for exactly what I paid, withouten any profit for my trouble."

Sure I felt sorry for him, but I was still mad and that wagon wasn't worth a penny over five hundred—five fifty tops—and there wasn't six hundred dollars' worth of pity in me. Besides, if folks were going to be telling the story about how Billy Floyd paid eleven hundred dollars for a wagon that was worth half the price, I sure as hell didn't want them substituting my name for his.

I shook my head and tried to move on, but Billy kept in front of me and blocked the way. "If you didn't want the damned thing you had no business looking like you did."

"I look any way I damned please."

"And another thing, you had no right trying to shame me in front of my boys."

"I didn't try to shame you."

"Yes, you did."

I couldn't answer because he was right. There wasn't a soul who knew Henry Sterret who wouldn't also know that the hitch on his wagon would never be busted.

"And don't think you fooling me now," he added. "You want that wagon so bad you can taste it, but first you have to jaw me down."

"That's enough," I said. Folks say I got a short fuse, but I swear it would take a saint on a day twenty degrees cooler not to lose patience with such a fool.

"All right," he called after me, "you had your chance. And don't come running to me next time you need somebody to do your work."

I kept walking because there wasn't anything else to do, but you could have boiled coffee on the back of my neck. I heard him say, "You boys stand right there and see nothing happens to our wagon."

There wasn't any question what he was going to do now. The ether had started to clear and he realized he owed eleven hundred dollars for a wagon he couldn't use if Henry Sterret had left it free and clear in his will. All Billy could do was approach every last soul who had bid against him and hope there was a bigger fool than him to take it off his hands. I could have told him that maybe God made some but not often. That's what I was thinking when the wife found me.

"Where have you been?" she said. "I've been looking all over."

"Take this," I said and handed her the pasteboard with my number.

"Where are you going now?"

"I got an idea."

I found Beulah on the front steps of her house, chin in the palm of one hand, sitting spraddle-legged like an orphan. The straw hat was hanging down her back and her hair had turned frizzy with the heat.

"I want you to do something," I said.

"What?"

I said it again.

"What can I do?" Damned if she didn't have a pretty smile, even if maybe it wasn't hers.

"Billy Floyd paid eleven hundred dollars for Henry's flat-bed wagon."

"What?"

She wasn't going to get the best of me. I ground my teeth and repeated it.

"Someone told me," she said.

"Beulah, you and I both know that wagon ain't worth but maybe half that."

"I don't know any such thing."

It was a wonder the way her hearing improved when there was a dollar sign in front of the words. "I'm not going to argue about what you know or don't know," I said. She cupped her fingers round her ear. "I want you to go to Ferris and tell him you made a mistake. The wagon shouldn't have been put up for bid. You had already sold it to me."

"I thought you would want that wagon," she said. "You should have bid. I wouldn't be surprised if you couldn't talk Billy into selling it to you for not much more than he paid. He never struck me as being greedy."

"It ain't his greed I'm worried about."

"What?"

I let it pass and went on. "You go tell Ferris and I'll give you six hundred dollars."

"What about Ferris's commission?"

"I'll pay that too."

"Six hundred is a long way from eleven, even with the commission thrown in."

"It's a hundred more than the wagon is worth."

"What?"

"Are you going to talk to Ferris?"

"I couldn't do that. It's against the rules of the sale. If you want that wagon you're going to have to deal with Billy."

The way she would tell it, I came to her to beat Billy out of his wagon and her out of five hundred dollars.

I went back down to the barn, taking a wide turn so I wouldn't have to look at the damned wagon. By the time I started back to the house, people were loading the things they bought into their pickups, crossing back and forth like it was moving day at the insane asylum. I saw the wife marching across what used to be grass but was now just trampled-down green dirt.

"Ferris getting near the pie safe?" I asked.

"I already bought it."

"How much?"

"I settled up. Why don't you bring the pickup to the gate and I'll help you load it?"

If she had got it cheap I wouldn't have had to ask. If I pressed her she might tell me, but she sure as hell would blame me for not being with her.

I backed the pickup to the gate and damned near knocked into Billy, then jumped out of the cab to be sure he was all right.

It was a brand-new Billy Floyd who was smiling at me, not grinning but smiling. It sure wasn't the man I'd left awhile back. It wasn't even the man I had seen standing under the catalpa with his boys. Unlikely as it seemed, I guessed he had found a bigger fool than himself, so when folks told the story about Billy and the wagon they would have to add that there was at least one other in the world and it didn't take Billy long to find him.

"Who did you sell it to?" I asked. I wanted to know only to be sure to stay clear of the man.

"Didn't."

"Didn't?"

"No, sir. I asked around but didn't nobody want it."

Then what are you so damned happy about? I wanted to ask it so bad I could feel the shape of the words in my mouth.

"I see the missus bought that pie safe," Billy said.

"We're going to load it in the pickup."

"No need for that. I got a wagon. Me and the boys will haul it for you."

What's that old saying? If you fall in a pile of manure, might as well go in the fertilizer business.

The wife came up to see what the delay was about, and I told her Billy was going in the hauling business.

"You folks are my first customer," he smiled.

We walked to the top of the grade that led to where Billy's boys still kept watch over the wagon.

"Mind you don't scratch it," the wife said. "I don't want it bouncing around."

"We'll handle it like it was a baby. I got a blanket somewhere in my pickup to wrap it in, and we'll tie it down. The boys can ride in back to be sure it don't slide."

We walked a few steps down the grade, then Billy called to the boys. "Hi, Rich, Bobby. Come up here." They started up the slope, carrying their boxes of contents. "Put them boxes down," Billy yelled. They stopped and stared at their father to be sure they heard right. "Put them down I say. We got us a job of work to do."

The wife supervised the loading of her pie safe on the wagon. I wandered back to the pickup. I could hear Ferris still singing, but there was only a handful of folks left. Beulah sat on the steps of her empty house, still spraddle-legged and with her chin in her hand. The pull string from her straw hat made a red line along her neck.

When the wife finally came I backed the pickup to the road so she wouldn't have to walk through the pasture again in her good shoes. I drove about a mile, waiting for her to say something. She knew I was waiting, so she waited too.

"What do you reckon got into Billy?" I finally said.

"Can't imagine." I knew without looking, from the way she said it, she was smiling.

"You going to tell me?" I demanded.

"Not if that's the way you ask."

We rode another mile. Hell would freeze before I asked her again.

"Beulah talked to him."

"What?" I said. She spoke so soft I wasn't sure I heard. That got her laughing so hard it was another mile before she could talk at all.

"Beulah spoke to him."

"You said that."

"You know Beulah. Why are we slowing down?"

"So I can hear what you have to say. When you finally get around to saying it."

"Well, right after I bought the pie safe I went to find Beulah. She was standing with Billy. They didn't notice me, but I could hear them. 'I see you got Henry's wagon,' Beulah says. Billy has that hang-dog look. You know the way he does. Beulah just goes on with what she has to say. 'As far as I'm concerned, I'm glad it was you and not some stranger.'

"'They were laughing at me,' Billy says. 'They're still laughing.'"

"Never mind about that," I said.

"Beulah had that look in her eye."

"What look?"

"Watch the road," the wife said. "I don't know how to describe it. She goes along from one year to the next without really saying anything, then suddenly her eyes change and you know this time she means what she's saying and you better listen up. 'I talked to a man about shipping my car down to the new place in Florida,' she says to Billy. 'You know what he told me it would cost? Five hundred dollars.'"

"Five hundred dollars?" I exploded.

"That's just the way Billy said it," the wife laughed. "Don't you see what Beulah was doing?"

"For five hundred dollars I'd drive her car from here to Alaska and back."

"So would she and she never drives anywhere but around town. I have no idea what the man told her, but I know it wasn't any five hundred dollars."

"What's this all about?" I asked.

"I'm getting to it."

"Eventually."

"Billy tells Beulah that he'll carry the car for her. 'The minute I heard you got the wagon I thought of that,' she says. 'Since I'll have to pay such an outrageous sum, I would much rather it be to someone I know than to a stranger.'"

"So she's picking up where Henry left off," I said. "No wonder Billy was smiling when I almost backed the truck into him. I'd be smiling too if I was in his shoes."

The wife shook her head and pursed her lips like she does whenever she has something important to say. "Billy actually took his hands from the bib of his overalls," she said. "His shoulders straightened and you could see the load coming off. 'You and the mister, rest his soul, always been more than square with me,' he says. 'And that's a mighty fine thing you're offering to do for me. It ain't that I don't appreciate it. But I just can't accept. Not this time. I'll be glad to carry your car for you, but I won't take a penny more than expenses.'"

"You sure that's what he said?" I asked.

"I was standing right there."

"It just don't sound like Billy."

"I heard it with my own ears."

I didn't say a word to her about talking to Beulah.

When we got home the wife started fixing supper. I poured some whisky in a tall glass over ice and moved out on the porch to cool down and wait. About a mile off I could see a cloud of dust, which was probably Billy and his boys bringing the pie safe. It was too far to be sure. I drank a little and ran the cold glass back and forth across my forehead.

Maybe the wife thought there was something different about Billy now. Like there was no knowing what he might do next. In my book that made no sense. He was a Floyd, and it was just like one of them to turn down five hundred dollars from a woman who had more money than brains. You would never catch me acting like Billy. Or like Beulah neither.

Personally I wondered how long it would take for Billy to get tired of being in the hauling business. I would be willing to take the wagon off his hands when he did and pay him what it was worth, minus wear and tear of course.

HARDLY WORKING

It was nothing special for Buddy to drive Clay Dixon to the coast. Buddy was always doing things for Clay, and this time it wouldn't even be out of Buddy's way.

Clay was meeting Janet Ann, the latest of his lady friends, and would drive home with her. That was fine with Buddy because on the way back he would have the Econoline Clay sold him packed solid with fresh fish. If he was going to get them delivered in good shape there would be no time to waste.

For as long as Buddy could remember, his family had worked for Clay Dixon. Which also wasn't unusual, because it seemed like everybody worked for him. When you own four farms in two counties, plus the Old Dominion Auto Exchange, the Spee-dee Laundromat, the Dairy Queen, the Kayo gas station, the Silver Screen drive-in movie, and you're a director of Carter County State Bank, and you live in Sterlings Draft in western Virginia, it's simple logic that nearly everybody in town would be on your payroll.

Right from the start, Buddy Campbell was something special and Clay treated him different. Even before Buddy could walk, his mother took him with her when she went to clean the Dixon place, trying to please whoever was the current Missus Dixon. Buddy would earn a nickel every time he said something that sounded like Clay.

"Hear that?" Clay would shout. "He can't hardly say mama, but he knows he'll get a nickel if he says my name."

Buddy was a big baby, with rolls of fat around his wrists and knees. He had his mother's soft blue eyes and his father's gentle nature. His hair was almost pure white, like an old man's.

Clay owned just two farms then, and Buddy's father worked

them for him. They lived in the tenant house on the home farm. Clay rented the other farmhouse and tenant place to a series of people who came and went with the seasons.

"I treat folks fair and square," Clay said. "Is it too much to ask that they do the same for me and pay their rent on time?"

By then Buddy was earning twenty-five cents a bucket picking berries, wild strawberries from the side of the hill above Clay's house, blackberries from the other farm, and raspberries from the third farm when Clay acquired it. Later Buddy earned dollars helping with the haying.

He lost his baby fat and became slim and hard. He still had his mother's eyes, but the planes of his face were like his father's, as though they had been molded separately, then brought together and forced to fit. His hair stayed almost white but grew so thick you had a feeling he could stand in a hurricane and it wouldn't muss.

The same year Clay bought his fourth farm and Buddy was thirteen, Buddy's father took off for Roanoke in the pickup one Saturday and never came back. Three months later Buddy's mother got a picture postcard showing a panoramic view of Helena, Arkansas, with the legend, "Land of Opportunity."

"Am feeling well," Buddy's father wrote. "Hope you are the same. Love to the kids. Will write later." But he never did. The card had been mailed from some place in Colorado that began with B. You couldn't make out the rest of the postmark.

The only turning point it marked in Buddy's life was that he, his mother, and two sisters had to move to a smaller tenant house. For more than a year Buddy's mother hadn't worked because of her heart. She had no strength for anything and was always out of breath. The doctor told her she shouldn't smoke, but she could no more give it up than Clay could quit chasing women. Clay arranged for her to get on the welfare and later, when she got worse, for the county nurse to come out once a month.

Buddy didn't replace his father as man of the house because the real man had always been Clay Dixon. His decisions weren't consistently on the mark, or even consistent, but they were final. If he got down on a person, a choir of angels couldn't get him to change his mind. So if he fired you, there was nothing to do but leave town and start over again. But as long as he liked you, and you did what he told you, he took care of you.

Even his wives continued to live in Sterlings Draft and work for him after they were divorced. Suellen ran the Dairy Queen, just like she did when she and Clay were married. Jeanette was in charge of the Silver Screen drive-in, and Pauline managed the laundromat, her son by her first marriage running the gas station. Clay's own sons, Bobby and Clay junior, worked the farms. Clay had his headquarters at the Old Dominion Auto Exchange, where Buddy worked. Once you were a member of Clay's family, there was no way out unless you crossed him so bad you left him no choice. That applied equally to the folks he hired and to his real family. Of course he made money from all his businesses, but you had the feeling that if he didn't he would sooner let them die than sell them.

Friday morning Clay told Buddy about driving to the coast, which meant the old man had had a session with Janet Ann the night before and let her take his car. When Buddy pulled up to the house on Saturday, Clay was still eating breakfast. He came to the door with a fork in his hand, a paper napkin tucked in his belt. He was a big man, with a deep chest, short arms, and ham hands. His eyes were round and deep, alive like a professional poker player's. His mouth wide, with vise-like lips, and his teeth the color of fresh tanned leather from years of smoking legions of cheap cigars in his plastic holder. Lately he had taken to dressing like a cowboy, cord pants with a wide belt and silver buckle, yoked shirt, string tie, held in place by sterling silver clasped hands, narrow boots that had to pinch his toes, and a genuine Stetson ordered from a store in Dallas. The outfit Janet Ann's influence. She was big on cowboys. The boots made him walk funny, like he was forever about to step in a pile of dung but couldn't stop himself in time.

"Just be a minute," Clay said. "Come on in and help yourself to coffee." He waved his arm and the fork ran down the screen door.

"Just finished breakfast," Buddy said. He knew if he went in the house Clay would sit for an hour, telling stories and handing out free advice, or detailing his latest adventures with Janet Ann. Then he would blame Buddy for being late getting started. But Clay could tell a story. If just half of what he said about Janet Ann and him was true, it would whip someone half Clay's age. "I may go any time," he had told Buddy, "so I already ordered the casket and told the undertaker to leave room in the lid, because whenever I go it's going to be with the bridge up and all flags flying."

Buddy turned the van around, backing carefully to the rim of the big muddy hole that would eventually be a swimming pool. Clay had set deck chairs around the edge of the hole, so he could watch the men working. No one could ever say that Clay Dixon didn't enjoy every dollar he made, or deny he did it all himself.

His advice showed the kind of man he was. "Listen, son," he said to Buddy, "you're selling used cars in a town where you know everybody and everybody knows you. You got to stick it to your friends because your enemies won't never give you the chance." Cast-iron balls, folks said, and Buddy admired him for it, wishing he could be the same. Clay had started with less than nothing, just like Buddy, and had made something of himself.

Clay finally emerged from the house, slapping on his cowboy hat, then pushing it to the back of his head. He carried a canvas suitcase that he slid behind the passenger seat.

"Working hard?" he asked.

"Hardly working," Buddy answered.

It was Clay's standard greeting, and the response never failed to delight him.

Clay pulled himself into the van, and Buddy turned in front of the handsome brick house, then rolled down the steep driveway, slowing at the curve and gunning the engine up the rise to the road.

"You seeing the Packard girl?" Clay asked.

"Off and on."

"It's one or the other," Clay said. "Never both."

"She's in Blacksburg at the university most of the year."

"Where you ought to be, instead of selling used cars for me."

Buddy hoped Clay wasn't going to start that again because any fool could tell he didn't mean it. He had never gone past sixth grade himself and it hadn't stopped him. Besides no member of Buddy's family had ever seen the inside of a university and he didn't think it was up to him to be the first.

"You ought to see more of the world," Clay said.

"I aim to before it's over." That ended the subject as far as Buddy was concerned and he was relieved to see Clay seemed to agree.

"I figured you was going to visit the Packard girl at that camp her folks have at the coast, and me and Janet Ann and you and her could get together and have some fun."

"I'll be heading back just as soon as I load up," Buddy said.

Clay undid a button of his shirt and reached in a finger to scratch his chest. "Load up what?"

"Fish. I'm guessing blues should be running this time of year. Along with sea trout and maybe some early crabs."

"What in the world are you going to do with a load of fish?"

"Sell them. It was your idea. You said—"

"I never did," Clay protested.

"You said that what we need around here is some fresh fish."

"When did I say that?"

"You said it."

"You opening a fish market?" Clay asked.

"I already contacted Joe Chalky at the country club and Mr. Hon at the Hong Kong Dragon. They'll take all I bring them."

"I sure as hell don't remember saying nothing about fish," Clay said. "Sounds crazy to me."

"That's what people said about you when you were starting out," Buddy said.

"That was different," Clay insisted.

Buddy let the subject rest. Clay had a hundred money-making ideas a week, but he didn't like anyone picking up on them, especially if they had a real chance of success.

"Fish," Clay snorted. "Craziest idea I ever heard."

If Buddy had any doubts about the plan, that laid them to

rest. Then he remembered that when Clay asked you to do something for him, he liked for it to be special, something out of the way. Meeting Blanche Packard was possible under the circumstances, but a business deal definitely was not.

"Actually, I wasn't going to start until next week, or maybe the week after, but when you said you wanted me to carry you to the coast I figured I might as well kill two birds with one stone." That took some of the curse off combining his own business with doing Clay a service, but didn't cure it.

Buddy had lain awake nights deciding how he could fetch fresh fish from the coast without their going bad. He made a couple of trips and talked to fishermen from Deltaville to Cobbs Creek. He lined up an ice house nearby and checked the advantage of block ice against chipped. Then he started putting money aside, a little each week, until he was ready. If he could pull the thing off, he calculated he could double his money every trip. By the end of a year he could have a whole fleet of trucks, real refrigerator jobs, running back and forth from towns all up and down the Shenandoah Valley and be raking in money by the basketful. Everything hinged on this first trip, because if it wasn't a success he was wiped out and probably wouldn't have the courage to try it again.

Before they had crossed Afton Mountain and reached Albemarle County, Clay was into his latest bout with Janet Ann.

"I swear, if I live to be as old as Methuselah I won't understand women. I tell her I'm building the swimming pool for her. You think she's grateful? Or says, 'Thank you, honey, that's mighty nice'? In a pig's kazoo. She gets a look in her eye, like she put something in her mouth and don't know whether to swallow or spit it out, and tells me, 'Look, Mister Clay Dixon, you want to build me a swimming pool, you put it in my yard, not in yours.'"

Buddy smiled sympathetically and nodded. He could hear Janet Ann saying those exact words. She wasn't much more than half Clay's age and she knew how to give him hell.

"So I tell her that wouldn't make no sense," Clay continued.

"For one thing, there ain't room. Not for the kind of pool I'm building." He picked the cigar from the plastic holder, dropped the butt out the window, unwrapped a fresh cigar, and leaned forward to light it, then examined the glowing tip. "Know what she says? 'Then build a smaller one.' Can you beat that?" He removed the cowboy hat and ran a hand over his bald head. "One thing you got to say for Janet Ann, she gets the last word." He held the hat against the sun to read the roadside signs. "Why did you drill them holes in the side of the van?"

"To let the water out when the ice starts to melt," Buddy said.

"You really mean to bring back a load of fish."

Buddy nodded. He knew Clay was trying to make the whole idea seem foolish, because that's the way he operated with other people's schemes and he couldn't stop himself even when dealing with Buddy. But knowing what Clay was about didn't prevent a small cloud of doubt from blocking the sun for a moment.

"I'm going to need a pit stop pretty soon," Clay said. "You rushed me out of the house so fast I forgot to go to the toilet." He needed to stop again outside Richmond and once more when they reached West Point.

"Where you staying?" Buddy asked.

"The Rip Tide Motel," Clay said. "They know me there. I been coming every season for the past ten years." His voice bright, then fading to an almost inaudible whisper.

"You feeling all right?" Buddy asked.

"Just tired," Clay said. "I think I'll close my eyes a spell." But when Buddy pulled into the Chesapeake Diner at Shackelfords Clay was wide awake. "Why are we stopping?" he demanded.

"Need gas," Buddy said. "Might as well eat at the same time."

"You get the gas. I'll pick up some hamburgers and pop. We can eat on the way."

"What's the rush?" Buddy asked.

"Son, when you got a woman like Janet Ann waiting on you, eating lunch is the last thing on your mind."

By the time Buddy had paid for the gas Clay was back in the van. "I got you a cheeseburger, an order of french fries, and a Coke," he said. "You owe me a buck seventy-five."

"Where's yours?" Buddy asked.

"I ate while I was waiting for your fries." He wiped his face with a handkerchief and fired a fresh cigar. "I don't remember when I seen it this hot in May. A month from now Janet Ann will be thanking me for building her that swimming pool. You mark my words."

"You can smell the ocean," Buddy said to change the subject.

"There's only one thing I can smell, and it ain't the sea air."

Buddy slowed to a crawl as he pulled behind a farmer driving a tractor between fields.

"There ought to be a law against them things on a public highway," Clay said. He leaned far out the window to see around the tractor. "I reckon you can pass. I don't see nothing coming."

"There's a double line," Buddy said.

"I see it," Clay snapped, "but if you don't get around him we'll be another hour getting there."

The farmer moved onto the shoulder of the road and waved them past. "About time," Clay said. "Now put this thing in gear and let's get going."

As they entered Deltaville, Clay straightened his cowboy hat and adjusted his string tie.

"You want to stop at the IGA for anything?" Buddy asked.

"Janet Ann takes care of that," Clay said. "She'll have the drinks poured and a plate of crackers and a cheese ball waiting for me."

Buddy drove to the end of the road, then turned left onto a sand and clam-shell drive. "I don't see your car," he said. "You want me to stop?"

"She probably got tired waiting and went for a little drive. I'll check the office to see what room we're in." Clay jumped to the ground and reached back for his canvas bag. "You go on about your business."

"Can't do anything for another hour or two," Buddy said.

"Suit yourself," Clay said and headed for the office at the center of the row of weather-stained doors.

The neon vacancy sign was already on, though barely visible in the glare of the mid-afternoon sun. Buddy had a feeling the sign was never turned off. There were four cars pulled in front of rooms with jutting air conditioners that dripped onto the clam-shell walkway. Metal numbers on the doors were speckled green. Buddy wondered if anyone, except an occasional tourist, ever spent an entire night in the place.

He heard a screen door slam, then saw Clay shuffling across the drive to the van. He seemed to have aged twenty years in the few minutes since Buddy watched him go into the office. Clay's face was gray and even in the shadow of the cowboy hat the skin beneath his eyes sagged. The whole cowboy outfit suddenly looked ridiculous, as though an old man had decked himself in a costume. The boots that made him walk peculiar now made it almost impossible for him to walk at all, forcing him to set one foot before the other in mincing steps. His bag hung from one hand. With his other he tried to stuff a sheet of paper into his breast pocket.

He opened the door of the van and slung the bag behind the seat, then pulled himself in. He tried to unwrap a fresh cigar, but the cellophane wouldn't come loose. Finally he lost patience and threw the cigar on the ground.

"What happened?" Buddy asked. It wasn't that he didn't know, but he couldn't accept that it was happening to Clay Dixon. He had heard plenty of stories about how young women treated old men, but none of them applied to Clay, who could get all the women he wanted, and when he was tired of one there was always another.

"She ain't coming." Clay smoothed the sheet of paper across his knee, then balled it and tossed it out the window.

"She sick or something?"

"How the hell should I know?"

"What did she say?" Buddy asked.

"She ain't coming. You deaf or something?"

"What about your car?"

"She says she'll get it back to me." He pulled out another cigar, managed to get it unwrapped and stuck in his holder, but his hand shook so bad he burned his fingers on the match before he could light it.

"What are you going to do?" Buddy was thinking of his load of fish and whether Clay would demand that they head straight back to Sterlings Draft. But Clay was thinking further down the line.

"What can I do?" he sighed. "You go on about your business and don't pay me no mind."

Buddy drove back to town and stopped at the IGA for a couple of cans of High Life, but Clay wasn't interested. Buddy didn't want to load the fish too soon and be forced to drive through the heat of the day. It would be a long slow ride, with the van almost riding on the axles. Probably take eight hours, maybe more. At least he had made arrangements with Joe Chalky and Mr. Hon to accept the fish no matter when he got there.

He drove the narrow road to Cobbs Creek between fields of hip-high corn or tall marsh reeds, where the ground was too soft for planting. The few farmhouses were raised on blocks, the open space beneath them covered with painted lattices. Bethel Baptist Church had a sign announcing a tent revival for early June.

Clay slumped in his seat, the cowboy hat tipped over his eyes. He could have been asleep, except that every couple of minutes a cloud of cigar smoke erupted from his mouth.

One side of the ice house at Cobbs Creek had a faded advertisement for Red Man Tobacco, the One to Chew for Flavor. It was still too early to load ice, but Buddy decided to go ahead and take his chances on it melting because he felt sorry for Clay and figured he would want to get back to Sterlings Draft as soon as possible.

Buddy helped slide thick blocks of ice onto the floor of the van, shaving the edges until they fit perfectly and made a smooth surface. Then he drove to the dock, cut his deal at Cobbs Creek Fish, stepped past whole families of sleek cats to the long wooden table where three men were gutting fish, then flipping them into barrels. They paused every few minutes to hose the table and wash the fish intestines into other barrels. The cats waited patiently, but overhead gulls wheeled and swooped.

The price was three cents a pound more than Buddy expected, but the few crabs they had were thrown in as a bonus, so that evened things. It was working out pretty much the way Buddy had planned it.

When the fish were weighed and Buddy paid for them, he headed back to the ice house for chipped ice to lay over the load. Every time a door opened, some fish slid out. Buddy caught them, hosed them off, and threw them back. A trickle of water had started to flow through the vent holes in the sides of the van. He got down on all fours to examine the springs and see how close they were to the axle. It would be all right if he didn't hit too many bumps. Everything would be lighter as the ice melted and ran off. Of course that would mean the fish were closer to spoiling. It was what Clay would have called a trade off if he had been paying attention, but he still sat slumped in his seat, puffing his cigar.

They doubled back to Deltaville, driving the worst stretch of road when the load was heaviest. The van was bottom and top heavy at the same time. Every breeze seemed to catch it and move it across the road.

Once they cleared Deltaville and the road was smoother and wider, Clay seemed to shake himself awake. He pushed his hat back and reached for a fresh cigar. "It don't hardly seem possible that something that stinks so bad can taste so good," he said.

Buddy was glad to hear him say anything.

They rode a few more miles in silence, but Clay was drumming his fingers on the dash, the way he did when he was thinking of something. "I bet you're getting hungry," he said.

It meant that Clay was hungry, which was a good sign as far as him getting over the disappointment of not meeting Janet Ann, but a bad sign as far as the health of Buddy's fish was concerned.

"There's a place along here that serves the best crab you ever had. Me and—I come here all the time."

"I'd be afraid to stop," Buddy said.

"Them fish ain't going to spoil. Hell, you got enough ice to drive from here to Panama."

"It's awful hot," Buddy said.

"All the more reason to stop now and wait until the sun goes down."

That made no sense, but Buddy was not in the habit of arguing with Clay.

"There it is. Over there on the left. Captain Crab." Clay pointed. "Pull over quick. If you miss it, you have to go half a mile before you can turn around."

Buddy parked in the shade of the cinder-block building and examined the van before following Clay into the restaurant.

A dozen men and women were seated on benches at long wooden tables. Sections of newspaper were spread in front of them, and between each couple was a bucket of crabs.

"Wait until you get your teeth into these beauties," Clay said. "You'll be thanking me for the rest of your life."

Clay ordered for both of them, then dove in as soon as the crabs were served, attacking them methodically, big claws, small claws, and body, which he cracked open.

"Eat up, son," Clay said. "When these are gone we'll get more."

"Maybe we should get back on the road," Buddy suggested.

"Plenty of time. Stop worrying about them damned fish. You only live once, so you might as well enjoy it."

Before they left, Clay had eaten a bucket of crabs and part of another. He reached for the check, pulled out his gold-rimmed aviator glasses, and added up the columns of figures to be sure the waitress hadn't made a mistake. "Might as well split it," he said. "Your share comes to eleven dollars, plus a dollar for the tip, and another buck seventy-five for what I laid out for lunch. Let it be thirteen fifty and I'll let you make me for two bits."

"I'll have to pay you next week," Buddy said. "I'm running a little low on cash."

Clay had to stand to get his fingers in his pocket. He pulled out a roll of bills and counted off a twenty. "You got a couple of ones?" he asked Buddy. "I ain't got no change."

The sun was almost down when they returned to the van, but it was no cooler. Melted ice poured from the vents, turning the gray sand black. Clay stuck a cigar in his holder.

"Now, tell me honest, wasn't them the best crabs you ever ate?"

"Yessir," Buddy agreed. "Very tasty." He put the van in gear and pulled onto the highway.

Clay kept talking about the crabs until they reached West Point, where he fell asleep. Just before they reached Richmond he woke.

"These boots are about to kill me," he said. He leaned forward and raised his foot, then groaned in pain and slid to the floor beneath the dash.

"What's the matter?" Buddy asked. "What happened?"

Clay groaned again and clutched his chest. "My heart," he gasped. "I'm having a heart attack." He tried to push himself back into the seat but the effort was too much.

Buddy pulled off the road, ran around the van, and opened the door on Clay's side. Clay started to fall out, but Buddy grabbed him in both arms and set him on the seat. I should have known, Buddy thought, all them stops, him looking so bad, and then Janet Ann not showing up.

Clay's cowboy hat had fallen off and was on the floor. His whole body was drenched in sweat that showed through the cowboy shirt, his face deep gray with heavy beads of sweat on his forehead.

"You got to get me to a hospital," Clay moaned. "I'm dying."

"I'll get you there," Buddy said. "Just hold on. I'll get you there as fast as I can." He slammed the door and ran around to his side of the van. Water was pouring out the vents and he felt guilty for thinking about the possible loss of his fish when Clay was having a heart attack.

Then Clay made him feel worse. "I know you're thinking about your fish. You probably got every cent you own tied up in this deal. I'll make it up to you. Just get me to the hospital and don't let me die here on the road."

"I'll get you there," Buddy said, "but I got to stop to get directions." He had to stop twice more before he found the hospital and pulled into the emergency entrance.

The next hour ran by on a whirr of words. The doctor asking him about Clay's medical history. Then a nurse asking the same questions. A woman with a nest of hair asking all sorts of questions about medical coverage and next of kin. Buddy answered the best he could, but there was a lot about Clay Dixon that Buddy discovered he didn't know.

"I'm going to put him in intensive care so we can run some tests," the doctor told Buddy.

"He's going to be all right?" Buddy asked.

"I doubt he's in immediate danger, but we'll know more after the tests."

Then Clay's voice, thin and watery, "Is that you, Buddy?"

"Yessir."

"Let me see you."

Buddy pulled a curtain aside. Clay was lying on a stretcher. His clothes had been removed and were piled between his legs. A sheet covered him to the waist. His color was better, but there were plastic tubes in his nose. A bottle of clear liquid hung over his head, with a tube hanging from it and taped to his arm.

"You want me to call your family?" Buddy asked.

Clay smiled faintly and his eyes rolled up in his head. "Which family you mean? My former wives or my no-good sons? All of them waiting for me to kick the bucket so they can carve up what it took me a lifetime of work to put together. You're the only family I got. I always treated you like you was flesh and blood, and you can't deny it. Stand by me now in my hour of need." He reached out a ham hand, clamped it on Buddy's arm, and kept it there as an orderly wheeled the stretcher down the hall and onto an elevator.

At the door of the intensive care unit, a nurse told Buddy to stay in the small waiting room at the end of the hall. "Don't worry, Clay," Buddy said, "I'll be right here all the time."

The door closed noiselessly behind Clay and Buddy wandered down the hall. Through a large window he could see the lights of the city. He didn't know what floor they were on, but he was sure it was higher than he had ever been. There was something exciting about being able to see an entire city and watch the headlights of cars moving far below him. Then he reminded himself why he was there, which automatically made him think of the load of fish now surely rotting in the hospital parking lot. He wouldn't make any money on this trip, but at least Clay would see that he wasn't a loser.

He dozed in a deep plastic-covered chair. The doctor shook him awake.

"Vital signs look good. His blood pressure is high, but he says he has medication to control it. I'm going to move him to a room and let him get a good night's sleep, and we'll run more tests in the morning."

"He won't die, will he?" Buddy asked.

"Not tonight," the doctor said. "Why don't you get yourself a room for the night and check with us in the morning?"

"If you don't mind, I'd just as soon stay right here. I can stretch out on the couch if I get tired. I promised Clay I wouldn't leave, and I don't want him waking up and finding me gone."

Sunlight poured past him. People moved about but no one seemed to care that he had spent the night on the couch. He unfolded his legs and swung them to the floor. When he tried to stand he fell back and tried again. He recalled there was a nurses' station at the other end of the hall and around a corner. His neck hurt, his back was sore, and his legs were not working properly, but he made it to the nurses' station and was told Clay had been taken to a room two floors below.

When he found the room, he hesitated at the door, then tapped it so lightly no one could possibly hear. He pushed the door open, and there was Clay, sitting up in the bed, wiping the corners of his mouth with his thumb and forefinger, a breakfast tray over his lap.

"Working hard?" Clay said.

"Hardly working," Buddy answered automatically. Then, "How you feeling?"

"Never better," Clay said. "I'll say one thing for this place, they got comfortable beds and the food ain't half bad."

"What about your heart attack?"

"False alarm. I bet it was them crabs, one of them must have been bad."

Buddy immediately thought of the ruined load of fish in the back of his van. With the sun up and all the ice gone, the smell would be pretty high by now.

"The doctor says they want to do more tests."

"To hell with that," Clay said. "With what they charge here I could stay in the finest hotel in the world or take one of them Club Med cruises Janet Ann is always wanting me to go on. See if my clothes ain't in the cabinet." He hopped out of bed, the white hospital gown flapping open behind him.

He pulled on his clothes, then searched the room for anything he could use, stripping a pillow case and dumping in a small tube of toothpaste, a toothbrush still in its plastic holder, a towel and washcloth, a packet of Kleenex, and a plastic bottle of hand cream. Then he emptied the water pitcher and dropped that in, along with the tray it sat on and a heavy glass.

"Where's my hat?" he demanded.

"I reckon it's still in the van."

"It better be. I paid fifty bucks for that sucker, and you can bet somebody will hear from me if they lost it."

Clay handed Buddy the bulging pillow case and headed for the stairs.

"We could take the elevator," Buddy suggested.

"And let them catch us?"

"You mean you ain't paid the bill?"

"Look, boy," Clay explained, "if I'd of died they wouldn't of got nothing from my family. So why should they complain that they don't get nothing just because I'm still alive?"

The odor from the van was like a solid mass. Clay waved a hand in front of his face, then fit a cigar into his holder. "I'll tell you one thing, son," he said, "if anybody ever took a mind to steal this thing, it wouldn't take no Sherlock Holmes to track him." He found his cowboy hat on the floor and brushed it before putting it on.

Buddy could afford to smile because if he hadn't made anything for his trouble, at least he wasn't a loser. But what with driving out of his way and the fish costing more than he planned, he had to borrow ten dollars from Clay for gas.

"That runs it up to twenty-three fifty you're into me for," Clay said. "I swear I don't know what you would have done if I hadn't come along."

Buddy mentally calculated what the fish had cost, plus the ice, and subtracted what he owed Clay.

"Just what do you aim to do with them fish?" Clay asked.

"I hadn't thought," Buddy said. "I figure since they're yours as much as mine, it's up to you to say."

"What the hell do I want with a load of stinking fish?"

"Last night you said—"

"I never said about paying for rotten fish that ain't good for nothing but fertilizer. Hell, all I got to do is walk into any pasture and get all the fertilizer I need."

"You said—" Buddy protested.

"What I said, and if you think real hard you'll remember, was that it was a crazy idea. I tried to warn you it wouldn't work, but you wouldn't listen. There wasn't enough ice for you to drive around the block, much less all the way from Cobbs Creek."

Buddy clamped his mouth shut and pursed his lips. His fingers tightened around the steering wheel.

"And don't be taking on like it's my fault," Clay added. "A man got to learn from his mistakes. If he don't, then he's a damned fool."

And that's a fact, Buddy thought.

When they stopped in front of Clay's house Clay pulled his canvas bag from behind the seat, then leaned back into the van. "You can forget the twenty-three fifty you owe me. It was worth that much if it taught you a lesson."

"Yessir," Buddy answered. "It did that."

Buddy turned the van around and headed into town, but

everywhere he drove the sickening odor of dead fish surrounded him, as though it would be a part of him for the rest of his life. He could hear folks telling stories about Buddy Campbell and his stinking fish, laughing at him, having their fun at his expense. He could make up the lost money, but once folks started laughing there was no end. And Clay would be the one laughing loudest.

All my life I looked up to you, Buddy thought, but you're a small man, Clay Dixon. A small man in a small town. All you ever done is take advantage of people. Use them as long as they were useful to you. You're a rank stranger to everyone. You got no family now because you never had one in the first place. Your ex-wives work for you because that's all they ever done. Your sons hate you because you're their boss, not their father. You put my mama on the welfare, but you always made damned sure you got your rent check. And you make a big deal about how good you always been to me. But I been a damned sight better to you than you ever been to me.

I ain't even sure you had a heart attack, or if it wasn't just your way of getting back in control after Janet Ann threw dirt in your face. You even cheated the hospital that was trying to save your life. Then stole things from them you can't use and don't want.

But the worst part is that you'll never change. You don't even know you're a rank stranger and that you'll be that way until you die, an old dog who knows all the tricks. But just once in your miserable life you got to see that you can't tell everyone the sun is shining when it's pouring rain.

No, that ain't the worst. The worst is that I wasted all this time trying to be like you, when I can't think of one reason why I would want to.

Buddy kept driving until he was in the mountains, where he could be alone and could think. What would Clay do, he asked himself, if it was him instead of me? A man got to learn from his mistakes. That's what Clay said, and he was right. So first I got to stop thinking like a Campbell and start thinking like Clay Dixon.

He watched the sun set and waited for it to be dark. Then waited some more. When he was sure Clay had gone to bed, he started back to town.

At the end of Clay's driveway he killed the lights, coasted down the short grade, made the turn, then eased past Clay's house and around the side. The hole for the swimming pool gaped like the open mouth of a sleeping giant.

When he opened the door of the van the odor of dead fish filled the night. In the barn he found a pitchfork.

It took thirty minutes to get all the fish in the hole. Then he sat in one of Clay's folding chairs and rested.

"They're all yours," he said. "You told me you would take them off my hands, so I delivered them. You might not like what you bought, but you can't argue about the price."

He picked up the pitchfork, carefully replaced it where he found it, and drove away.

The only thing he regretted was that he wouldn't be there in the morning to see Clay's face and hear him say, "I can't understand why Buddy would do such a thing to me. I always treated him fair and square, like he was a member of the family."

But in his heart he would know. In his heart he would know.

THE HEART OF DONALD DUCK

Ever since Ben McLeod returned from his honeymoon some piece of my memory has been gnawing at my understanding. Part of it was easy—the part about Ben, his family, and Donald Duck. It was the rest I couldn't quite get straight. Then last week, at Rita McLeod's birthday party, the missing pieces fell in place.

I had always been accepted as almost a member of the McLeod family. Ben and I grew up together. His father loaned me money so I could take advantage of the scholarship I was offered by the University of Virginia. Then he used his influence to see that I was hired to teach history at VMI. Protecting his investment, he said. And after I retired Ben saw that I was offered a job as curator of the Stonewall Jackson house.

I used to own the farm next to Ben's. He had twelve hundred acres of rolling valley land. I had seventy-two acres of rocks. But Ben always had his tenant care for my twenty Herefords as though they were his own and never charged me. Ben's first wife, Lily, died five years ago and he and I became even closer. Then last year he married Rita Mills, a woman half his age. He didn't ask my advice, so I didn't give it.

What I remembered about Donald Duck were the special movie shows for children on Saturday afternoons. Ben or Lily drove the boys to the theater and picked them up when the show was over. This was long before VCR's, when television was new in our part of Virginia and showed "I Love Lucy" and "The Flying Nun" and wrestling programs. The Saturday movies were vintage films that had been spliced together a thousand times, probably the same ones Ben and I saw when we were kids. There was a full-length adventure, serials with Buck Rogers or Tom Mix, and the usual assortment of cartoons, Bugs Bunny, Porky Pig, Mickey Mouse, and Donald Duck. For some reason no one ever understood, every time Donald Duck came on the screen the younger boy, Willard, covered his eyes and screamed so loud his brother had to take him out to the lobby until the cartoon was over.

Ben and Lily tried reasoning with the boy, but how do you discuss anything with a child who was then no more than five? Might as well tell a drunk that he ought to give up drinking.

At my advice they bought a large stuffed doll of Donald and put it in the children's second-floor playroom. The doll looked friendly enough and had an interesting quack, neither belligerent nor threatening, more like a dyspeptic lamb. The idea was that Willard would become familiar with Donald and lose his fear. A rational approach to an irrational problem. My plan succeeded but not for the reason you might suppose.

Willard would not at first go near the doll. At night he closed the door of the playroom, and the next day he waited until his brother opened it. During the second week Willard would play alone in the room but at night he still insisted the door be closed.

One Friday about a month after the doll arrived Ben and I were in his downstairs office. He was packing his gear for the opening of deer season, trying to talk me into coming with him, as he tried every year. I didn't bother to dissuade him because he had never killed anything more dangerous than a fifth of bourbon and most years he never saw a deer. He couldn't find his hunting knife, the one that had been his father's. We looked under papers and boxes, then checked the desk drawers. Lily had warned Ben repeatedly to lock the knife away so the boys wouldn't hurt themselves, but as usual he never got around to it. Without alarming her, he started searching, determined to tan someone's breeches as long as Lily didn't find out why.

We found the knife almost immediately in the children's playroom under one of those three-legged stools grown-ups think children like. The blade and crosspiece were covered with what looked like shreds of cotton batting.

Ben followed the cotton trail across the floor. On his hands and knees he found Donald under a chenille spread that covered a worn-out couch. The doll's face was smiling sweetly, but its body was flat, almost stripped of its stuffing. The way Donald's belly had been reduced reminded me of something I almost remembered. We heard Lily's voice in the hall, so Ben wiped the knife clean, shoved it in his pocket, and raised his finger to his lips.

Two weeks later, when I came to dinner, Ben had forgotten his precautions and was explaining what I had already seen. We were eating in the kitchen, as we always did, sitting on metal-tipped chairs so as not to scar Lily's precious slate floor. Every time I looked up from my plate I saw her collection of blue-flow china and antique vases.

"You know how Donald's stomach stuck out and sort of sagged like Sheriff Klock's?" Ben asked. "Well, Willard had made that doll look like it had been Klock's prisoner for a month and had to eat that slop the sheriff serves instead of food."

"How do you know it was Willard?" I asked because once Ben starts on the sheriff there's no stopping him.

"Had to be," Lily said. "Nat was under my feet in the kitchen all morning."

"The seams along the doll's stomach were opened so carefully only the thread was cut," Ben added, as though the way the doll had been opened explained who did it.

"What did Will use to—?" Lily started to say, then gave up. She obviously had asked the question before and never gotten an answer.

"At least the boy dealt with his fear," Ben said quickly.

Ben was right but he was never one to ask why. That's one of the differences between us. I connect things, look for the meaning within the meaning. What I had been trying to remember had to do with the cotton batting on the playroom floor. I had been studying some old letters by members of the Stonewall Jackson Brigade and their battles with the Thirty-eighth Indiana Regiment, the Hoosier Tigers. I'm not sure what I had in mind, except that it seemed to relate to Willard and his battle with Donald Duck.

"In the winter of sixty-four," I said, "the Stonewall Jackson Brigade was under Jubal Early, who was defending the Valley against General Sheridan."

Ben took a deep breath and rolled his eyes at Lily.

"Conscription had broken down, and there were plenty of desertions."

"It's all in the history books," Ben said to Lily. He had this habit of talking to me through her.

"Not this part," I said. "There are only half a dozen letters and a couple of diary entries." I paused to let the significance of what I was about to say sink in, but no one seemed to notice. "It was a particularly cold winter and the Hoosier Tigers had cotton-filled vests. That's what reminded me—"

"He's going to slander Virginia's fighting men," Ben said. "I feel it in my bones."

Lily stood and began to clear the table. "Were they the ones who burned our house?"

"That was the One Hundred and Thirty-eighth from New York," Ben said.

Lily piled the dishes and began to carry them across the kitchen to the sink. "I can never keep them straight."

"Are you going to let me tell my story?" I asked.

"Couldn't stop you with an elephant gun," Ben smiled.

The telephone rang and Lily winced as Ben scraped his chair across the floor to reach the instrument against the wall. I waited impatiently while he listened for a moment. "It's for you," he said to Lily. "Muriel Money."

Lily turned off the water and wiped her hands across her apron. "I bet it's about the garden club."

I waited.

Lily covered the mouthpiece with the palm of her hand. "Our speaker has the flu. Could you substitute?" she asked me. "You could tell them about the Hoosier Panthers."

"Tigers," I insisted.

"Next Tuesday. One o'clock." She uncovered the mouthpiece. "He'll do it. He has some story about the Hoosier Panthers." She listened for a moment. "I know. But what can you do at the last minute."

So I told the ladies of the garden club about the Indiana regiment, and they were no more interested than Ben had been. "The Hoosier Tigers had a special chewing tobacco called Hart's Delight," I said. (The ladies looked properly revolted, though everyone knew half their husbands chewed.) "The package had a heart dripping blood on the cover. The Tigers carried the tobacco in the breast pocket of their shirts. What happened was that after every battle there was a burial party, with men from each side searching for their dead and wounded. When the men from the Stonewall Jackson Brigade found a dead Tiger they quickly cut his breast pocket and stole his Hart's Delight. When they got back to camp they would announce they had the Heart of a Tiger. It was a kind of joke. At first the men cut only the pocket, but later they got careless and cut out a piece of the dead man's flesh. And as time went on they cut deeper until they came close to telling the truth about having the Heart of a Tiger. And they weren't always too careful about stealing only from the dead."

As I spoke Willard and Donald Duck dropped completely from my mind. I seemed to be talking about Ben and me. He became a Hoosier Tiger and I was picking at his bones. I had it wrong, of course, because I was connecting things before there was anything to connect.

God knows Ben wasn't perfect, but it seems to me in his second marriage he deserved someone different from the woman he got. I don't mean to criticize Rita, if he had married her first I could as well say the same about Lily. I have this theory about second marriages. The first time out we try to change the other person. But in second marriages we try to change ourselves.

When you looked at them, the two women were nothing alike, except that no one had ever accused either of them of letting something go with a whisper when a shout would do. Lily had been a big blowsy woman with steel-gray hair she plaited and pinned in various shapes behind or across her head. Rita had a bony face with deep blue eyes set in skin that looked like watered milk. Lily's bosom had been generous. Rita's was small, even for someone as slight as she was, and her waist could be circled by two hands. Ben always said Rita had to stand up twice to make a shadow, which may not be original but is accurate. She had a way of flicking her straight blond hair to clear her head or maybe make a point. But there was nothing vague about her. Maybe that was what Ben saw in both her and Lily, because Ben was never a strong person like his father and needed all the help he could get.

I had introduced Lily to Ben, and I was with Ben the day he met Rita. We were on our way to town for a slow dinner and a meeting of the Horse Center Commission. Rita was trying to change a flat tire.

I might as well pause here and explain the commission, which becomes important later. It was one of those committees who seem to appoint themselves, or let the county do it, to accomplish good works. In this case it was to improve tourism—everyone is in favor of tourism—and perhaps generate a little local industry.

The commission had no power, which translates to no money. Our job was to prepare a report and present it to the county. The county would study what we wrote, then present its report to the governor, who in turn would study the county report, make changes, and perhaps put a request for funding by the legislature in the following year's budget. If by some chance the governor actually asked for the money, the legislators had enough reasons to turn him down.

Back to Rita. It was a winter afternoon, one of those days

with ragged cirrus clouds, yet raw with a threat of snow. She was on the New Providence Road, past Miller's Mill, looking cold and helpless. We stopped, of course, and offered to help. The first thing I noticed was a gash in the pillow of flesh beside her thumb where she had cut herself with the pointed end of the lug wrench. Then Billy Floyd and one of his endless number of sons pulled up and also offered to help. Trust Billy to remember that Ben was probably the softest touch in the county. Ben gave Billy ten dollars to change the tire and drive the car to Ben's farm while he bandaged Rita's cut hand. He took her arm, but she pulled away.

"Who are you?" she asked.

When your family has been in the county from before the Revolution and you have one relative who signed the Declaration of Independence—look it up—and another who served in Jefferson Davis's Cabinet you might think people would know who you are. "Forgive me, Miss—" in his gallant voice because his pride was hurt.

"Missus." Her tone said that everyone made the same mistake. "Missus Herman Mills." Then more friendly, "Rita."

Rita sounded like someone from an old Fred Astaire movie, but she didn't look to me to be more than sixteen.

"Ben McLeod," he said.

Of course she knew who he was. Everyone in the county knows Ben McLeod, at least by name. "Very pleased to meet you," she said and held out her good hand. I drew a simple nod.

"I have a little farm the other side of Sterlings Draft. I thought I would take you there, tend your hand, and wait for Mister Floyd to bring your car."

And she knew the size of the McLeod farm down to the last rod. We discovered quickly that her former husband had driven her past it one day and calculated how many lots could be squeezed into McLeod's twelve hundred acres, allowing for roads and a small shopping center.

"That's my place there," Ben said. We turned off a dirt road onto a macadam surface. "I had the county put down blacktop because the dust was driving Lily crazy," he said, then paused a moment. "Lily was my wife. Died five years ago."

"My husband died last year. Heart attack. Went just like that."

She didn't sound too grieved.

The house is a copy of the place the Yankees burned in sixty-four, a bulky brick and clapboard building with chimneys at its four corners plus more chimneys at what had once been end walls. Lily had redecorated the rooms one at a time, sewing the drapes herself and saving the scraps to make scatter rugs. Lily's pride, however, had been the kitchen with its polished slate floor, and her collection of antique vases and blue-flow china.

While Ben bandaged her hand Rita chattered. "You could do a lot with this place," she said and continued as though Ben had asked her what she had in mind. "You ought to get rid of the shelves with those jugs and dishes. They block the light."

"My wife was a collector," he said quickly, explaining why he kept Lily's things, not defending her taste.

I was so fascinated with Rita's effrontery that I failed to see that she was already competing with Lily. "If it was me," Rita said, "I would take out the whole wall and put in sliding doors." She flicked back her hair. "Herman and I—Herman was my husband—we had this old house we were fixing up. He was going to sell it, then buy another with the profit. Herman could do anything, put up wallboard, fix plumbing, add a roof. He even knew about electricity. When we got back from our honeymoon I had cards printed. The H and R Construction Company. For Herman and Rita. Get it? I gave them to him for his birthday. Then he dies."

She never described Herman, then or later, except by his attributes, but it was clear to me that he was one of those real estate blow-hards who live in some vague future, skip the de-tails of the present, and ride around in an impressive car that is never paid for. In my view the marriage, the house they were remodeling, and the man's death were a series of mounting deficits. But Ben had already compared himself to Herman and discovered his own deficiency.

"Herman worked for that old crook, Jesse Carter. I work there too," Rita said.

Ben heated water and spooned tea into Lily's best teapot.

"Carter is on the Horse Center Commission," I said so Ben would be able to identify him.

"I expect he is," Rita said.

Then she told us about driving past Ben's farm with Herman and dividing the place into lots. Suddenly her voice grew small, her words ran together. Ben had to lean forward to hear. "Herman was going to do it after you"—she almost whispered—"died." She flicked her hair again, her voice stronger. "Because he said your sons wouldn't want the responsibility. And now look what happened."

As far as I could tell, her husband's dying was the best gift he could have given her, but Ben didn't see it that way. Fortunately Billy Floyd arrived with Rita's car and saved Ben from having to defend himself for having outlived Herman. So Ben gave Billy another ten dollars as a kind of reward.

Because he gave Billy twenty dollars to change a tire it did not mean that Ben was a free spender. He arrived in this world with enough money, and it looked like he would leave it with more than he began. He had twelve hundred acres—eleven hundred ninety-six—mostly in Red Delicious and Stayman Winesaps. But he also kept a herd of Charolais and was experimenting with Rambouillet sheep. The cows and sheep were Lily's idea. Ben would have been perfectly happy to stick to his apples, but she had this notion that he should restore the McLeod farm to the three thousand acres it had once been. Ben dug in his heels—land prices were too high, he didn't want to go into debt, the right farms weren't for sale. In the end he bought two relatively small neighboring farms he could easily afford and he put in the cows and sheep.

It didn't take much persuading to get Rita to stay for supper, and I accepted Ben's tepid invitation that I join them. After supper Ben and Rita sat on the loveseat that faced the fireplace in the parlor and Ben built a fire. He found the bourbon where he hid it from himself behind Lily's nested iron skillets and added a touch more liquor than he might have if he had been drinking with me.

"I love an open fire," Rita said. "It's so romantic."

I finally excused myself, borrowed one of Ben's cars, and attended the Horse Center Commission meeting. He obviously had other business in mind.

Women find Ben attractive. He is a tall graceful man whose elegance had been a source of embarrassment until his body thickened and he seemed to earn his good looks. His smile is warm and generous. In all his pictures his pale brown eyes stare frankly forward, and his brown hair, flecked with gray, curls from beneath his Texas hat. When he takes it off, you are surprised to see that the top of his head is stone bald, with a ridge down the center as though the halves had been welded together. His nose is an axe blade, straight and sharp, except for a little bump near the bridge, like someone had honed it poorly.

He looks more erotic than he is, as a number of women, some even while Lily was alive, had discovered. Frankly I am much sexier and I'm a bachelor, but I'm not given the chances that fall to him.

After thirty days he asked Rita to marry him, as though he felt he had to do something before her warranty ran out. He had meant to surprise her, but it was he who was surprised when she accepted on the spot. Immediately he worried if either of them was doing the right thing. He worried what his sons would say. He worried that he was being disloyal to Lily. He worried that he wouldn't be up to Rita, a woman half his age. But most of all he worried that Rita would compare him to Herman.

Right after the ceremony and the reception I drove Ben and Rita to Roanoke for the first leg of their flight to Hawaii. Ben said he always meant to return there after serving on Admiral Buller's staff during the Second War, but Lily swore she would never take an airplane just to fly to some foreign country. Rita, whose first honeymoon was a long weekend at Virginia Beach, was happy to go anywhere he chose.

HARDLY WORKING

Their troubles began as soon as they returned to Sterlings Draft. Rita wanted to remodel the house, not one room at a time the way Lily did, but all at once, attacking as though the house were an enemy position, which of course it was. Ben approved, like a new recruit who doesn't know what he's doing but can't wait to get started. "It's more than fixing an old house," Rita said. "I feel like I'm building a new life. I never had the chance with Herman." Perhaps she meant that Herman had died too soon, but I felt she meant something more.

"You're good at it," I told her. "You have the knack."

What she lacked was taste, but Ben straightened her out. He helped her pack up Lily's antique vases and blue-flow china and move them to the barn because he never liked the things in the first place. And he let her replace outside walls with sliding glass doors. But when Rita wanted to throw out the Hepplewhite sofa and the Sheraton chairs he drew the line.

He gave her a lecture on George Hepplewhite, with an explanation of his light graceful furniture and compared it with Thomas Sheraton's use of straight lines and graceful proportions. All of which Ben had looked up and memorized at Preston Library at VMI. Maybe Herman wouldn't have been able to talk about eighteenth-century English furniture, but the words had the same blow-hard quality that I took to be Herman's trademark.

Having lost the Hepplewhite battle, at best a pyrrhic victory for Ben, Rita next attacked Lily's holy city, the kitchen. Ben had already cooperated in removing the collection of china and vases, so perhaps Rita thought she would have more success.

She called in men with jackhammers and had them remove the polished slate floor. She moved the sink from one side of the room to the other, replaced cabinets, built a cooking island, had ovens set in a brick wall that had to be braced with steel beams in the basement. Ben seemed as anxious as Rita to get Lily out of the house. Then he came home and found that Rita had moved to the barn his perfectly good Hot Point refrigerator and Kenmore dive-in freezer, his only household purchases since Lily's death. In their place Rita had installed a two-thousand-dollar eight-foot-high refrigerator freezer.

Ben walked up and back, trying to open its false cabinet doors, while she explained its features. "The best thing is that it's no wider than the cabinets. You don't even know it's a refrigerator."

"Is being a refrigerator a secret?" Ben opened and closed more doors that turned out to be freezer compartments. "You don't throw away perfectly good appliances," Ben muttered.

"There are fans to prevent food smells from spreading." The explanation had turned desperate. "You never have to cover anything."

"You could buy a lifetime supply of Tupperware for two thousand dollars," Ben said. "The freezer is still under warranty." That was pure Herman, going back to the days he and Rita had been fixing the old house they meant to sell.

Tears welled in her eyes. "I want us to start fresh with new things for a new life."

"You don't start fresh by throwing away good appliances." Ben turned to me. "She would have thrown out the Sheraton and Hepplewhite if I hadn't stopped her." This was maybe the tenth time he had told me about the furniture. Even Herman probably never worked that side of the street so hard.

I offered to take the Hot Point and Kenmore off his hands. My refrigerator and freezer could stand replacing, as long as the price was right.

"If you want to buy something," Ben said, "take this goddamned contraption Rita bought and I'm going to have to return." It wasn't the money, as it would have been with Herman. Ben had already spent a fortune remodeling the house.

Still Rita did not give up. She discovered that Lily and I had often ridden together. Over the years I have continued to keep horses and I still ride. So it was no surprise when Rita appealed to me to teach her riding. Not dressage or anything fancy, she just wanted to be able to stay on the animal's back.

Teaching Rita wasn't easy. To start with she had a bad seat, her fingers clutched the reins, and she made the horse as afraid of her as she was of it. But every time she fell off she got back on, I'll say that for her.

One night Ben and I came home to his house from yet another meeting of the Horse Center Commission and found Rita studying an old photograph of Lily standing with her hunter, Pistol Pete. A ribbon was clipped to the horse's headpiece and Lily had turned the horse's head so you could almost read the lettering. Pistol Pete had his mouth open and it looked as if both he and Lily were smiling for the camera.

"She looks like the horse's mother," Rita said.

There was an equine quality to Lily's face. I had noted it years before, then stopped seeing it as I grew used to her, or maybe when she put on weight and her face filled out.

"Am I prettier than her?" Rita asked.

"Much." Ben hadn't married either one for her looks, but that was too hard to explain.

"Why did you marry her?"

At this point I should have excused myself, but neither of them seemed to notice that I was still there.

"I don't really remember," Ben said. "It was a long time ago." He seemed to dread her next question and said something about remodeling.

"Stop trying to change the subject." She took a deep breath. "Why did you marry me?"

That didn't seem to be the question he expected and he fumbled the answer. "Because I loved you," he said.

"Loved?"

"I married you in the past tense," he said and made his blunder worse.

"And you loved Lily too." She tossed her hair.

"You were married to"—he couldn't say Herman's name—"your first husband."

"The reason I married Herman is that he looked like he had a future," she said.

Suddenly I knew the question he had expected her to ask. The words seemed to ring so loud in his head that they made his eyes water. He had been waiting for her to ask why she had married him. In his mind a question that had no answer he could accept. It was obvious he had no future, not the way Herman had. Herman drove past Ben's farm once and split the land into lots and streets and threw in a shopping center. The man had vision, he could see through the present and create his future. Ben was simply a farmer. An old farmer. He had his apples and his cows and his sheep.

The Horse Center Commission had been taking more and more of our evenings. The group had some good ideas about how to develop the land. What it lacked was money to buy the acreage to get started, and the prospects for getting the money were about as good as a drove of fleas buying their own dog.

Finally Ben figured out what he knew Herman would have seen at a glance. If someone leased the land to the commission, say a couple of hundred acres, and that same someone owned all the land around the two hundred he leased, then that someone would be in the driver's seat when it came to development. No Horse Center no chance for a development, but with the Horse Center there was no end to the possibilities. So Ben set out to prove that if he wasn't as quick as Herman, he was at least as thorough.

The best farm in the county, after Ben's, was the Dunbar place, about three hundred acres of cleared land and another fifty in timber. Levi Dunbar had lost his sons in Vietnam, his wife was ailing, and he had a half-wit daughter. If you went back far enough the land had belonged to McLeod. So Levi was willing to listen when Ben came to him and offered to buy the place. Of course the price of beef being low helped Ben's case. But it's a long way from being willing to listen to something and signing a contract to sell it.

Ben insisted I come with him when he talked to Levi. I had known the Dunbars as long as I had known the McLeods and fought with Levi, as my father had, about repairing our fences. If Ben had told me he was trying to buy Levi's farm I would have begged off. At least I had the good sense to keep my mouth shut.

Levi pumped Ben's hand once, in country fashion. "It ain't the money," Levi said. "You're being more than fair."

"Then what is it?" Ben asked.

"After the war between the states your great-granddad sold the land to my great-grandpa. Got top dollar at the time. I figure that if a man pays top dollar it ain't right for his kin to sell it out from under him."

"But you're getting top dollar too," Ben said.

"And that's a fact. Just between us girls, the place ain't worth what you said." Levi reached down and picked up a handful of dirt, then let it trickle through his fingers.

"I'm not going back on my offer," Ben said.

Levi's bright eyes were without guile. "A generous one," he said. "No question about it." He clapped his hands together to remove the dust. "I couldn't get half what you offered if I threw in a free poke at the wife," he laughed. Then suddenly serious, "Not with so many folks selling." He stooped for another handful of dirt and let it run through his fingers again. "If I was willing to sell," he finally added.

"You think about it, Levi, and let me know."

There wasn't anything to think about. Levi was more than ready to sell, but he didn't want to be pushed.

"What's going to happen to him?" I asked as we rode away.

I think Ben wanted to tell me the whole story right then, but that would have spoiled his surprise for Rita. "He could buy a bigger farm," Ben said.

"But he won't," I said.

"No, he probably won't. But for a little while he can play at being rich." That could have been Jesse Carter or Herman Mills talking. It didn't sound like Ben McLeod.

As soon as word got out that Ben was buying land it looked like the whole county was for sale. With the price of beef scratching bottom, no one cared two cents why Ben was buying as long as he bought their place.

He ended picking up two farms the other side of Dunbar's, Jed Coggman's and the Mason brothers', about five hundred acres combined. But between Ben's place and the other farms were my seventy-two scrappy but very adjacent acres. You could say I was the hole in Ben's doughnut.

I owe the McLeods a lot and there was never any question that I would sell if Ben demanded, but I was determined not to kiss his ass while I did it. I thought Ben would pay any price I named, so I named a high one. It wasn't just the money, I flat out wasn't interested in selling.

"The land ain't worth a quarter of that," Ben said.

"We both know what the land is worth," I said. "We're talking about what you're willing to spend."

"I'm not going to pay through the nose."

I could have asked what organ he was willing to pay through. "All right," I said, "name your price." I still didn't want to sell, but I needed to know what the land was worth to him.

He gave me a figure about half what I asked, which was twice what the place was worth.

"I don't like being pushed," I said.

"Nobody pushed you to take my father's money for your education. Or the teaching job he got you at VMI. Or being curator at the Jackson house. And nobody pushed you to accept my man taking care of your cows. Or any of the other thousand things I've done for you over the years."

"Most folks would say that comes under the heading of friendship."

"Then under the heading of friendship I want your land."

Maybe it was what Herman would have said in the circumstances but again it didn't sound like Ben McLeod talking. Yet I had seen him do it to Levi and had not complained, so I had no right to complain now. He was offering more than a fair price, just as he had offered Levi, but I had to know why.

"In good time," Ben said. He pulled out his pocket watch and studied it as if it were a calendar. "I'm inviting you to Rita's birthday party, June twenty-first. I'll tell you then." He continued to study his watch. "She's going to be thirty. Do you remember what it was like when you turned thirty?"

"What about my horses?" I said. If you break a man's routine he'll ask any number of stupid questions.

Ben laughed. "Under the circumstances why don't you give them to Rita for her birthday?"

"I'll sell them to her," I snapped.

For the party he had the Lincoln Town Car cleaned inside and out. I can't imagine why Lily let him buy it twenty years before. In all that time it had less than thirty thousand miles on it.

He waited until we had eaten, the waiter had brought Rita's birthday cake, and everyone in the restaurant had joined in singing Happy Birthday. Then he quietly made his announcement.

"You what?" Rita said. Folks at other tables couldn't help but overhear her.

"You now own more land than any woman in the county, maybe in the state."

She wiped her mouth before she spoke. "Thank you," she said. "Thank you very much." She wiped her mouth again. "When do I take title?"

"When I die, I guess." He paused to let her get used to the idea of being the biggest landowner in the area. "I haven't told you the best part."

She kept herself from asking.

"I offered three hundred acres to the Horse Center Commission. Free. I even told them I would pay the closing costs. That puts the horse center right in the middle of our land. Of course we'll be prime contractor on the horse center itself. I already filed papers for the B and R Construction Company." He paused again and was disappointed when she didn't react. "I got an architect working on the plan. The way I figure it, there will be the horse clinic on the left." He pushed his plate aside and set the sugar bowl where the horse clinic would be. "Then the administration building." He put the cut-glass flower vase with its plastic tulips next to the sugar bowl. "In the center we'll put two rings." He used the salt and pepper cellars. "With a judge's tower between them." I held onto my cake plate because I hadn't finished. "But the best part will be the indoor ring." He put his own cake plate in the center of the table. "The commission is talking about seats for a thousand, but I see places for five thousand. What the hell, if I'm going to do something why not do it right?"

How easily he slipped from "we" to "I." Exactly the way Herman would have done it.

"Beyond the outside rings I thought I would put the barn and an area for the competitors to have their campers. Horse competitors hate to pay fifteen cents for a real room." He glanced at me as though I was somehow responsible, or maybe he wanted to see if I was finished and he could use my plate for the barn.

"And that's just the horse center. I also been in touch with Holiday Inn about building a motel. And with McDonald's and Wendy's and Burger King." He was working up a head of steam, but he had run out of things to move around the table. "For the rest, I was thinking about houses on ten-acre lots with a lake in the center. And of course we build the houses."

His voice went on, the words tumbling after each other as though self-propelled. But I had stopped listening so I could watch Rita. Her eyes were cold and still. Tiny pearls of perspiration covered her upper lip. She licked at them with her tongue, then used her napkin. "What about your apples?" she said in a small voice.

"To hell with apples. I'm talking real money."

You rarely discover at what point a marriage fails, but it seemed to me that I could name the minute when Rita finally gave up.

"Tell me how this is so different from what you and Herman were doing?" Ben asked. He could say the name now.

"You think Herman and I were buying houses, fixing them up, and selling them because we couldn't think what else to do?" She took a deep breath and wiped her lip again. "We were doing it because we had no choice." She cut the cake on her plate into small pieces and mashed them together. "I didn't marry you to be the same as I was before."

"You can't change a leopard's stripes."

I didn't know if he meant himself or Rita. But I suddenly remembered the Hoosier Tigers.

"Spots. Leopards have spots. Tigers have stripes," she said.

I saw the smiling face of Donald Duck and heard his unhappy voice. His button eyes were watching me.

"What am I supposed to do with thousands of acres and a lake when you drop dead?" she demanded.

"I'm a long way from dying."

"That's what Herman said." She tossed her hair and seemed to stare past him.

Then I saw in Ben's eyes the look of the poor scared boys of the Stonewall Jackson Brigade. What had they been seeking when they stole the Heart of the Tiger? And why had they cut into the flesh of their enemies? Were they in some strange way staving off inevitable defeat by becoming the men they robbed? And what do you become when you discover you haven't taken the Heart of a Tiger but have stolen the heart of Donald Duck?

"I'm leaving," Rita said. She pushed back her chair and dropped her napkin on the table. I couldn't tell if she would be waiting for us outside the restaurant.

Ben paid the check and arranged with the waiter to box the rest of Rita's birthday cake and take it home. On the way out the headwaiter asked Ben if everything was satisfactory.

"Fine," Ben said. "Fine." Then he tried to smile, "Couldn't be better."

The following day I was at my old house, packing the last of my things in boxes when Ben stopped. He said he wanted to tell me something, so I climbed into his pickup and we drove across the fields. Finally he got down at a rise on what had been Levi Dunbar's farm and would now be the horse center. It hadn't rained for two weeks. The ground was baked raw. From a distant brake a single crow beat up, circled us, then disappeared. Ben stooped for a handful of dirt, as Levi had done, and let it slip through his fingers.

THE FAMILY MAN

All he needed was for Alma to come down pregnant. Not that Glenn didn't like her. She wasn't what anyone would call a beauty, but she kept herself nice. She already had two kids, so it couldn't be she didn't know which end was up. Two kids, a trailer, and a rust-bucket Mustang that even her second husband hadn't bothered with when he split.

Glenn swung his pickup onto a narrow blacktop road and instinctively ducked as water splashed from a pothole. It had been raining hard for two days with no sign of letup. After a wet spring the ground couldn't hold much more. The empty gun rack behind him came loose, and he reached back to straighten it.

Now he and Alma had one in the oven. If his wife Janice found out she would tell her brother, who would get some high-powered lawyer out of Roanoke, and Janice would end up with the house, the farm, the kids, the car, and everything else Glenn had put together over the past twelve years of damned hard work.

Glenn had done the bank a favor taking the ruined farm off their hands. Now, twelve years later, he had built a house, was ahead on the mortgage, and the farm was showing a profit. He wasn't about to throw his work away. Not for Alma Beauchamp or anyone else.

The solution was plain as the hand before your face. Alma had to go to Doctor Ferris in Richmond. Ferris had taken care of the Willis woman when she was going to have her seventh, her husband out of work and drunk. Even fixed her so she wouldn't have to worry ever again. Glenn had gone so far as to tell Alma he would pay for everything. All Alma had to do was agree.

He parked the truck on the soft shoulder of the road and felt the wheels settle in the rain-soaked ground. Water almost topped his boots as he herded the cows from the bottom pasture to safer ground.

By the time he returned to the pickup he was soaked. Across the road he could see the field he had sowed to alfalfa was flooded and spilling the seed down the incline onto the road in streams of blood-red mud. Rain poured down the neck of his shirt, drenching him from the inside out. He would have to change before seeing Alma and hope Janice didn't ask him where he was going.

At home he dressed quickly. Janice was still meeting with the church women. A problem avoided was a problem solved as far as he was concerned. Kitty, his older daughter, questioned him in her mother's place.

"Are you going out in this weather?"

"The only weather we got."

"When will you be home?"

"When I get back."

"Is that what you want me to tell mama?"

"Tell her to get out the kerosene lamps and the Coleman stove. It wouldn't surprise me none if the power went." He put on his coat and rain-soaked hat.

The child looked frightened and he tried to comfort her. "You like it when we go camping."

It was dark when he swung the pickup back on the road. He didn't really know Alma, he told himself. He knew where she lived, where she worked—the sort of thing everyone in Grayson knew about everyone else. He knew, for example, that Alma's first husband, Joe Lassiter, was killed when his truck jackknifed just before Christmas and Alma six months pregnant with Billy. She had meant to stop cashiering right after the holiday, but she stayed at the truck stop until the day foreman told her to get out before she had that baby in the cash drawer. She was back at work the minute she got Billy on the bottle.

Glenn also knew about Will Beauchamp, husband number two. Everyone in Richland County knew there was something wrong with him. But that didn't stop Alma from marrying him. Called himself a lay preacher, but there was a lot more laying than preaching. Come to find out later that was the reason he left Tennessee, where his people were.

When he skipped town everyone breathed a sigh of relief. Even Alma, because by then she had caught him out so many times that he had run out of interesting lies. He left her Claudie and not much else. But there must have been something about him because Alma never had a bad word to say about the man or what he done, stealing her money and taking everything that wasn't nailed down or too big to fit in the pickup she bought him.

Lights from the truck stop flared against the low sky, then vanished as the road dipped. To Glenn's right the creek that wound beside the road had spilled its banks. He would have to warn Alma not to take the Miller's Mill road home.

That was another thing. She had never once invited him to her trailer. The times they had been together they had met behind the Kinzel place, because old Kinzel lived alone, was part blind, and mostly crazy, and wouldn't anyone believe a word he said. Alma would leave her Mustang, get in the pickup, and they would drive up in the hills, where they did their business out in the open.

He couldn't even be sure how it all got started. He wasn't one of those men who go through life with his fly half unzipped. There had been a couple of times when him and his friends got liquored enough to carry on. Going out with Alma was nothing like that.

He smiled as he remembered Alma's blue chiffon dress at Marie Bynum's party. Marie gave the same party every year. The men stood in one room and the women in another. There was punch at one end of the dining table and ham biscuits at the other. Later there was ice cream, the brick kind with choc-olate, vanilla, and strawberry. At the last minute Janice decided not to go. Glenn thought that got him off the hook, but she insisted he go.

"That was her mistake," he said aloud.

Alma was the sort of company who helped with serving and made sure the ashtrays were empty and the dishes cleared. She was wearing a blue chiffon dress with short sleeves and a sort of bib that went from one shoulder to the other across her bosom. Every time she bent to pick up something the bib hung down and you could see about everything she had. She must have known all the men were staring down her dress, but the only time she smiled was when she caught Glenn looking. It seemed like for the rest of the night no matter where he put his eyes he was peering down Alma's dress. Later he started her car for her after she flooded the engine and followed her to the trailer to be sure she got home safe. He returned to Janice and told her how boring the party was.

The next week he went to the truck stop as if by accident. It was a warm spring night and there wasn't much doing.

"You look nice," Alma said.

He had put on clean pants and a fresh shirt. His flat face changed shape, became rounder, when he smiled. He nodded, and smoothed his sandy hair with his hand. He was no more than average height but seemed taller because of the way he carried himself.

Alma's uniform was too tight across the chest, so that the fabric gapped between the buttons, and she showed too much thigh when she swung her high cashier's chair around. She had pale blue eyes with tiny squint lines and dark red wavy hair that she pushed behind her ears.

Then he leaned over the cash register and suggested they go for a beer. "The girl who stays with the babies likes to leave early," she said.

"She can stay a few minutes this one time."

"I'll see if Mr. Bennet will let me off," she said.

They drove up the highway toward Jackson and stopped at a

place Glenn passed a thousand times. The beer wasn't cold, which gave them something to talk about, or at least got them started. Then in what seemed like no time at all they were back in the pickup, hugging and kissing and touching each other. Some kids drove by, honking their horn, and Glenn realized he had parked under a light. He jammed the truck in gear and peeled out of the parking lot. She sat close to him with a hand resting lightly on his thigh until he couldn't stand it anymore and pulled the pickup off the road.

It was she who insisted they get out of the truck. He remembered the old blanket he kept behind the seat and carried it under one arm, his other arm around her waist. The blanket smelled of oil and when he spread it on the ground he could feel flecks of something that he suspected might be cow dung. Her mouth covered his explanation as she pulled him to her.

From then on they met behind the Kinzel place but always drove to the same spot. When they finished, there was nowhere for them to go. Not just that he was married, but passion seemed to burn something out of them and they were left with nothing to take its place.

He picked his way through the rigs that crowded the parking area, found a spot behind the restaurant, and stopped beside Alma's Mustang. She wasn't at the register connected with the diesel pumps, so that meant Mr. Bennet had her working the cafeteria. It would be harder to talk to her there because the truck drivers were always wanting receipts for whatever they ate, even a cup of coffee.

The place swarmed with civilians and truckers. Kids ran everywhere, skidding on the muddy floor as they turned corners, running into folks and spilling drinks from paper cups. Old Jason was trying to mop the filth but it was a losing proposition. Glenn eased his way past the barber shop, the showers reserved for truckers, and the gun store. Alma was working the register like a piano, writing receipts for the truckers with one hand while she continued to ring up with the other. There were dark moons of sweat on her uniform beneath her arms, and the gaps over her bosom were bigger than usual. You could see the inside of her thigh without her turning. Her hair was frizzy and pushed out of place. A man who looked to be seven feet tall said something that made her laugh. But her fingers never stopped working the register and writing receipts.

Glenn fought his way against the tide leaving the cafeteria and stood behind her.

"I got to talk to you," he said.

"Not now," she said, then smiled at a trucker in a cowboy hat who was saying something about a flood in Wythe County.

"I need to know what you decided," Glenn said.

She glanced at the clock over the steam table. "I'll be finished in twenty minutes."

"Better get the chickens in, brother," someone said to Glenn and placed a heavy hand on his shoulder. "It don't get no worse than this."

He retreated to the front and hung around the news ticker, with its almost constant weather reports. "Flash flooding," someone yelled. The rest was lost in comments from the truckers.

The candy and souvenir counter was gutted. Even the magazine rack was empty. And there were kids everywhere, running, falling, shouting. Glenn drifted to the end of the cafeteria line, picked up coffee and a piece of blueberry pie, and wordlessly held out a dollar bill.

"Just a couple of minutes, honey," Alma said softly.

He nodded, and for the first time that evening noticed how flushed her face was and how it made her pretty in a little-girl way.

He sat at a table with a young couple and their baby. The man's hair was longer than his wife's and fastened at the back with a rubber band. The baby woke and began squalling. The mother continued eating while she tried to comfort the child. "Wants his dinner," she said to her husband. Glenn was so disgusted he could hardly eat his pie.

He made sure Alma saw him leave and waited for her in the pickup. It was raining so hard, water looked like it would come clean through the windshield.

When Alma scrambled into the truck and sat beside him she was out of breath. Her hair clung to her head and framed her face.

"Everybody's talking flood," she said.

"I seen worse."

"I should have worn a hat." She squeezed the palms of her hands against her head and water ran onto her shoulders and dripped to the seat of the pickup.

"Well?" he asked.

"Well, what?"

"Did you think about what I said?"

"Of course I thought about it." There was a catch in her voice. He refused to look at her in case she was about to cry. "I can't think of anything else," she added.

"So?"

"I told you I can't do it, and I can't."

"What do you mean you can't?"

"I can't." She turned to face him, but he was fumbling his shirt pocket for cigarettes. He pulled out a damp pack and offered it to her. She shook her head. "It would be like murder."

His hands trembled as he cupped them around the match. "That don't make sense," he said.

"I don't care what it makes." She tucked her legs under her. "To me it's taking a human life and that's a sin."

The windows of the truck fogged. It was like they were sitting in a lighthouse.

He pinched off the tip of the cigarette, set the stub on the dash. He decided to try another approach. "I wish there was some other way."

"I'm not going to talk about it." She folded her arms across her chest.

"You already got two," he said. "You need another?"

"It don't matter what I need. You got what you wanted, now I got to pay the price."

He knew she would get to that, as though he had taken something from her without giving anything in return. Which was all wrong. It was what he had given her that they were arguing about. And he could not resist a sense of pride that it was him who gave it. An image of her head thrown back and her arms gripping him so he could barely move flashed through his mind. That was something worth remembering, worth comparing with what his lovemaking with Janice had become.

"What are you going to do?" he asked.

"Don't you mean what are we going to do? I didn't make the baby by myself. You got responsibility."

"What can I do?" He turned the steering wheel back and forth like a child playing at driving. "If Janice ever finds out—"

"Don't give me Janice," she interrupted. "You weren't thinking about Janice when we were together."

"And you weren't thinking—"

"That isn't fair." She was crying now and did nothing to wipe away the tears. "Everything is my fault," she said.

"I told you what I was willing to do." He was trying to be conciliatory.

"And because I can't do what you want, you think that ends it. I could lose my job. And even if I don't, I'll have to take time off. It takes money to raise a kid."

"I know," he said.

"I bet that girl will want more if I tell her she got to change diapers and make formula."

"What do you expect from me?"

"And that's just the beginning. You know what dentists cost nowadays? And clothes? Hand-me-downs don't go but so far."

"If Janice ever finds out about me and you," he said, "she and her brother will pick me clean. There won't be nothing left but bones."

"I'm sick of hearing about Janice and her brother," she yelled. "You do what you want. It's what you'll do anyway." She shoved the door open. "Just don't bother me with all the reasons." She slid from the seat and slammed the door.

His throat was dry and he had to inhale four times before he could draw a deep breath. Alma was getting the short end of the stick, but that wasn't his fault. If she would just act reasonable and go to Richmond.

She yanked the truck door open and stuck her head in the cab. It was impossible to tell if she was still crying or simply wet from the pelting rain. "My damned car won't start."

"Get in," he said. "I'll drive you home."

He backed the pickup and turned the wipers as fast as they would go but they barely kept pace with the rain.

"You reckon it is a flood?" Alma asked.

"How should I know?"

"You don't have to take that tone."

"I'm sorry," he said. "I got a lot on my mind."

"We both do."

"You aren't responsible for the weather. Or that your car won't start," he added.

"But the baby is my fault. Is that what you mean?"

"It ain't what I mean."

"It's what you said."

"Stop putting words in my mouth."

"Which way are you going?" she demanded as he turned onto the road.

"Can't make it across Bryce Creek. Have to take the high road and double back."

"That's four miles further. The girl leaves at six sharp no matter what." She stared at the rain for a moment. "You really think it's that bad?" she said, trying to persuade him to take the shorter way.

The muscles of his jaw worked, as though he was trying to say something but couldn't make the words come loose.

"I didn't mean to snap at you the way I did," she said softly. "It's not many men that would offer anything."

Her words made him feel that he should have offered more. He wanted to do the right thing, but it never seemed to be enough.

"Don't be mad, honey," she said. "I hate it when you're mad."

"I'm not," he lied. Merely saying the words made them almost true.

"I thought I was taking care of everything."

"It was an accident," he said.

"None of them things is one hundred percent."

He nodded. It was easier to talk about how they had gotten into the mess than to figure out a solution.

Lights from the truck stop reflected in his mirrors became a dull glow, like the halos of cashiered saints. Alma leaned forward and wiped the inside of the windshield with her palm.

"Don't do that," he snapped. "It only makes it worse."

He almost missed the turn onto the dirt road at Crowders Fork, then hugged the hill side of the road, praying there were no other damned fools out on such a night. The pickup fishtailed and he heard Alma gasp. He leaned over the steering wheel, urging the truck up the incline.

"How can you see?" she asked. Her head almost in the windshield, she gripped the dash with both hands.

They were almost to the top of the hill, where the road bent sharply before beginning its descent. A stone came off the side of the hill, hit the roof of the cab, and bounced the length of the bed.

Then they saw it at the same moment. Where the road had been was a wall of seething mud, flowing through the branches of a pair of uprooted trees. It was as though there had never been a road beyond that point and the hill extended from its crest to the creek bed at its base in an uninterrupted line.

"Jesus Christ," he whispered. "The whole damned hill gave way."

"Can you turn around?"

"Not even in broad daylight."

"We could walk out," she suggested.

"Along the creek," he agreed. "That way is only half a mile."

Each waited for the other to move. "We got to get out your side," he finally said. "I'm tight against the bank." He reached beneath the seat and found a flashlight. When he tested it a yellow glow barely filled the cab. "Better than nothing," he said.

She opened the door and rain poured into the cab. "Shouldn't you turn off your lights?" she suggested.

With the motor dead and the headlights gone, there was a

feeling they had surrendered hope. The dim glow from the flashlight and the roar of the creek below them added to the desolation. He swung the light onto her to be sure she was still there, then followed her into the night.

The mud was ankle deep. Water sluiced past them, creating deep ruts. She grabbed his arm to steady herself and their feet slid together. When she glanced back at the truck, she looked like she wasn't sure they would be better off to risk the rest of the hill sliding down on them. "You reckon you ought to turn on your flashers?"

"Ain't no other idiots out on a night like this," he said.

He skated to the edge of the road, Alma clinging to him. "You ready?" he asked over his shoulder. Then without waiting took a step down. The flashlight flew out of his hand. He watched it bounce down the steep grade until its yellow light bobbed in the roaring creek before tumbling out of sight.

"Where are you?" Alma asked.

"Right here," he yelled.

"Where?"

Before he could say anything more she slammed into him, sending him further down the hill with her close behind. In spite of their perilous position he felt in control. Even Janice said he was a good man to have for an emergency. It was in the day-to-day things he wasn't so good.

The noise of the creek rushing downstream grew to a deafening boil. It was like nothing he had ever heard before. Not like water at all, but more like a herd of animals. Stones flew along the top of the water, then dove and came to the surface again. The ground quaked as though it were trying to retreat from the rushing water.

For a moment he thought that all he had to do was push her and the creek would do the rest. Then he struck the thought from his mind, tried to erase it. Killing Alma was no solution. It merely replaced one impossible problem with another.

"You all right?" he yelled back at her. At least all this bouncing can't be good for the baby, he thought. If she loses it that would be the end of the problem. But he wasn't sure he wanted it to end that way either. He wondered whether he wanted it solved at all if he was involved in the solution.

"So far so good," he said. "Now all we got to do is head upstream."

After they had walked awhile she asked, "How far you reckon it is?" Her breathing was short and harsh, the same as it was when they made love. "I can't go much more."

"Sure you can, honey," he said. "You can do anything you set your mind to." The words seemed to mean more than he intended.

When he thought they had gone far enough he veered from the creek. If they missed the trailer they would find what was left of the road and be able to retrace their steps.

They heard a child cry.

"It's Claudie," Alma whispered. "It's all right, baby, mama's here," she shouted. Then to Glenn, "Damn that girl, leaving them alone without even a light." Louder, as she realized there was no need to whisper, "Is the trailer all right? You don't reckon it slid off the blocks?"

He felt his way around the side. The sound of the crying child seemed to move with him. "I can feel the blocks with my foot. Might need some leveling after this is over, but that's all." He found the door. "The water grabbed your porch and steps. Open up," he shouted and pulled the door handle.

"Don't yell. They're already scared," Alma said.

The door opened a crack and Glenn pulled the handle out of Billy's hand. "Take it easy, son," Glenn said softly. "Your mama's right here. Everything's going to be fine."

That seemed to satisfy Billy, but Claudie cried louder. Glenn climbed over the doorsill and scrambled into the trailer on all fours. He leaned back to help Alma. The boys stood out of his way, not trusting him but unable to do anything about their mistrust.

Alma tried to scrape mud from her coat. "I'll get the light."

"Power's out," Billy announced.

"I'll get a lamp," Alma said. Claudie crowded close to her.

"Already got it," Billy said. "Out of kerosene."

"Then we'll use candles."

"Can't find any. Think we burned them all the last time the power went."

"You ever been camping?" Glenn asked the child.

"Sure."

"What's the first thing you do when it gets dark?"

"Build a fire."

"That's the second thing. First is to be sure your flashlight is handy."

Claudie stopped crying to put two fingers in his mouth and listen. "I got a flashlight," he said softly.

"Batteries dead," Billy said.

"Are not," Claudie answered.

"Are too."

"Why don't you get that light," Glenn said, "and see if the batteries work."

"I got one with good batteries because I take care of things and don't leave them burning," Billy announced.

"I take care of things too," Claudie said.

"Get both flashlights," Glenn suggested. "We'll see which is better."

They ran down the hall, each trying to be the first to find his light. "Don't run," Alma called after them.

Glenn sat on the floor, trying to unlace his boots, while Alma hovered over him. "I'm worried about the creek," she whispered. "It ain't never been this high. If it keeps coming the whole place could wash away."

Glenn loosened the wet laces enough to pull off his boots, then peel off his socks. "That creek ain't nowhere near here," he said. "We been moving away from it for almost fifteen minutes. The water outside is from rain. All you got to do is get out of them wet clothes and relax."

The light from the flashlight preceded the boys from the hall.

"See?" Billy said. "I told you his was all burned out."

Claudie was too close to tears to protest.

"You men have supper?" Glenn asked.

"No, sir," Billy answered.

"I reckon you're pretty hungry."

Claudie cheered up at the talk of food but became despondent when Billy pointed out that if the power was off, the stove was useless.

"I been out hunting plenty of times when it was wet and we couldn't build a fire," Glenn said. "You think we went hungry? Not a bit. I bet there's viennas and beans." Claudie nodded. "All we need is a can opener and I bet one of you knows where your mama keeps it."

"I do," they answered almost in unison.

"You get the food," Glenn told Billy. "And some plates. You find the can opener," he said to Claudie. "Reckon you can do that?" He motioned Alma toward the hall. She stood for a moment, undecided whether to do as he bid, then smiled and nodded before turning.

"Can we use paper plates?" Billy asked.

"Nothing better for camping on a rainy night," Glenn answered.

"You want us to open the cans?" Billy asked.

"Unless you know another way to get the food out of them."

They thought that was funny and shook the cans before setting to work opening them. Glenn resisted the temptation to help Claudie lift the ring in the top of the can of viennas.

"I found this," Alma said and placed a fat cream-colored candle on the oilcloth-covered table in the center of the kitchen. "I been saving it because it was the last thing Joe gave me before he got killed. I don't reckon he'd mind us using it on a night like this." She found matches above the stove and struck one on the underside of a cabinet, waited until the match flared, then lit the candle, revealing its colored map of Virginia surrounded by tiny dogwood flowers. Slanting through the map and wrapping around the candle were the words "Virginia is for Lovers," the O in "Lovers" in the shape of a heart. The handle of the tiny brass holder was bent out of shape. Alma tried to straighten it.

She had changed into a green housecoat with dark green buttons down the front. She hadn't bothered with trying to dry her hair but set it wet in large curlers. Her feet were in furry blue slippers. "Let me help with that," she said to the boys and moved to the kitchen counter.

"The boys are doing fine," Glenn said.

"There's a phone in the bedroom," Alma said. "You could call home so they won't be worried about you." She took down more viennas and beans, handing the cans to the boys to open, as Glenn moved down the hall. "That's Becky's father," she explained to Billy. "She's the one in your grade. His other girl is Kitty. She's two grades ahead of you."

The naming of his daughters made Glenn feel guilty that he had to be reminded to call. Worse, it brought back the fact that nothing had been settled between Alma and him. At least it hadn't been settled the way he wanted, which was the same as not being settled at all.

"While you're back there," Alma said, "you might as well get out of them wet clothes. There's a fresh shirt and jeans hanging in the closet. They was Will Beauchamp's," she added quickly, so Glenn wouldn't get the wrong idea about her having men's clothes. "He left them because they was in the wash."

At the end of the hall he opened the trailer's other door to check the rain. "Looks like it stopped," he announced as though he had personal responsibility in the matter.

"Thank God for small blessings," Alma said.

The phone was dead, which he accepted as another small blessing. He wasn't ready to have to talk to Janice and explain where he was, how he got there, what he was doing driving anywhere with Alma Beauchamp, or any of the other questions Janice would throw at him. Even she couldn't argue with the fact the phone was dead. Later he could explain how he happened to be at the truck stop, Alma's car wouldn't start, and it seemed only decent to offer to drive her home. The rest of the story fell in place. He rehearsed the words he would use while he washed, stripped off his wet clothes, and put on Will Beauchamp's shirt and jeans.

What would his life be like, he wondered, if he was married to Alma and it was Janice who was pregnant. The whole idea was impossible. Not his being married to Alma, but Janice being pregnant without first having a ring on her finger. Janice was a good woman, better than he deserved, and he wasn't sorry he married her. She was a good mother and kept the house spotless. She was a good cook, and no one could make money go further.

He hung his wet clothes on a rack he found in the bathroom and walked to the kitchen on bare feet. In the living room his muddy boots and wet socks were oozing red on the linoleum floor. Janice would have murdered him. He picked them up and started to apologize to Alma. "If you have some old newspaper to put them on," he said.

"Leave them and eat your supper," she said. "I'll clean up in the morning."

He set the boots down and joined Alma and the boys at the kitchen table. Claudie's head was bent over his plate and he seemed about to cry again. "I thought this was like camping out," he said weakly.

"It is," Alma assured him.

"We don't sit in chairs when we go camping. And we don't eat at a table."

"You're absolutely right," Alma agreed. She grabbed the candle and set it in the middle of the living room floor. "You bring the beans and viennas," she said to the boys. "Glenn will get the plates." She sat cross-legged and waited. "This is more like it," she said when they joined her. "Pass the viennas, I'm starved."

After supper Glenn told the boys about the time his father took him fishing on the Cheat River in West Virginia. In the flickering candlelight with the roar of the creek in the distance it was almost like they were on their own fishing trip. Somewhere in the middle of the story Claudie climbed in Glenn's lap, put two fingers in his mouth, and rested his head against Glenn's shoulder. "After we ate and the fire got low," Glenn said, "we would stare up at the sky. My daddy knew all the constellations, the Big Dipper, Orion the hunter, the Great Bear and the Little Bear. He showed me how to find Arcturus and how you follow the pan of the dipper to the polestar. You know about that, don't you?" Claudie nodded vigorously. Billy shook his head in slow wonder that any man could know such things.

"It's time for bed," Alma said.

The boys ignored her, and Glenn told them about deer hunts and the time him and his friend Bert Crosby got chased by a bear. Claudie fell asleep and Billy stretched out with both hands propping his head.

"They're asleep," Alma said.

"Am not," Billy answered and jerked himself awake.

"I just want to tell about the time I saw a fellow wrestle an alligator." But before he was well into it, Billy had dropped his head to Glenn's knee and slept.

Alma picked up Billy and Glenn carried Claudie to the room the boys shared. "I'll get them ready for bed," Alma said. Glenn nodded and set Claudie down.

How many times, he wondered, had Janice said the same words when they carried the girls up to bed? It was all familiar but somehow different. These were not his boys. He was only the father of the unformed baby Alma carried in her womb, but somehow that brought the boys closer. He tried to figure that out as he wandered back to the living room.

The empty cans were overturned and the paper plates scattered about. He started to pick them up, then stopped. It was the sort of thing Janice would expect him to do, but Janice would never eat from cans in the first place. If the Russians dropped the bomb and the whole place was going up in a mushroom cloud, Janice would have a hot meal on the table. There's nothing wrong with that, he whispered to himself. In a way he wished there was.

"Claudie wants to kiss you good night," Alma said.

He returned to the bedroom, but Claudie had fallen asleep. He kissed him anyway, then turned and kissed Billy.

Later he and Alma slept in her big double bed, she in her housecoat, he still dressed in Will Beauchamp's pants and shirt.

"I'd marry you in a minute," he said. His hands were folded

behind his neck, and he was thinking how much more he would like his life if it were true.

"No, you wouldn't," she said.

"How do you know what I would do?" he asked.

"You want your cake and to eat it." She turned onto her side to face him. "That's what life is all about, having your cake and eating it."

He started to interrupt but she hadn't finished.

"Except some of us don't never get the chance."

"That don't mean I wouldn't make a different choice if I could," he said.

"What you want is for things to be back the way they were." She rolled onto her back and closed her eyes.

"Stop telling me what I want," he said.

"Somebody had to say it." Silently she wiped her eyes with the back of her hand.

During the night he had to go to the bathroom. He checked his clothes draped across the rack. The best you could say for them was that they were less wet. Alma must have gotten up too, because when he woke there was a comforter over him. The power was on and he could smell coffee and bacon and hear eggs snapping in a spider.

His clothes felt clammy as he changed into them. The sun was shining, and through the bathroom window he could see the small porch about fifty feet from the trailer. The steps were nowhere in sight.

"What time is it?" he asked Alma. "My watch stopped."

"Almost seven." She had combed out her hair and changed into a cotton dress, but she still wore her furry blue slippers. A radio on the counter next to the stove played softly. She poured coffee into a mug and set it at the head of the oilcloth-covered kitchen table. "Eggs in a minute."

After he ate he pulled on his socks and muddy boots. "Should have put newspaper in them," he said.

She nodded.

At the door he put an arm around her waist and kissed her. "I'll come by as soon as I can and fix the porch," he said.

They both knew he was lying. She wanted to tell him not to bother, but it would have been too cruel.

He started the long walk back, wondering if the truck would be where he left it. He would have to back all the way down the hill. It would take some doing. One of the tires on the truck was worn almost down to the thread. He hoped he hadn't damaged it. And he wondered what he would say to Janice. That would take some fancy handling too.

THE HIRED MAN

Reid Stevenson III was an only child, the only one of his kind. His people were from Richmond, doctors, lawyers, accountants, dentists, specialists in what ails the world. They carried the city with them, creating it from one minute to the next.

When Reid was thirteen—an age when the Jews say a boy becomes a man—he was consigned for the summer to an aunt and her son, Reid's Cousin Ashley, at a summer place in Rockbridge County, in the western part of Virginia. At something under fifty acres, the place wasn't big enough to be a farm and too big to be anything else. Why Reid's uncle, Walter Snyder, bought it no one in the family could explain. But nearly everything Walter Snyder did was beyond understanding, which is a sort of explanation.

Poor Walter. He was a lawyer, but no one in the family trusted him to handle anything more complicated than a lease. Everyone could agree on that. And also agree that it was easier to feel sorry for him than be married to him. Reid's aunt, Maddy Stevenson, seemed to hate Walter for dragging her down with him. The summer place was the last straw. It was thirty miles from nowhere. She couldn't even get to the Homestead for a decent meal.

The reason he had been consigned to Aunt Maddy—Uncle Walter appeared only on weekends, arriving late Friday night and leaving Sunday afternoon—was that Reid's parents needed some time by themselves to decide whether they could settle their differences or should end them. Reid knew that he was responsible for those differences, and the more each of them assured him he was not, the surer he was. The ultimate threat, the one that pulled him back from sleep, was that he would have to choose between them. He tried to make a list of criteria.

When you came down to cases, there wasn't much to recommend either of them. Not when you compared them to parents he saw on television. It made him furious that he was being forced to choose and more furious to be told that he wasn't. But for all its seriousness, it was a recurrent anger rather than a constant. When you're thirteen, and have the constitution for it, there are plenty of things to worry you.

In other circumstances it would have been no hardship for Reid to spend a summer on the farm, but in other circumstances he would not have been given the opportunity. The house looked as though it had started out honest enough. Clapboard, lumpy from too many paintings, but carved cornices and wide windows, tin roof with chimneys at either end for fireplaces that had long since been blocked and replaced by wood-burning stoves. Beneath the roof peaks large round carvings that looked to Reid like Amish hex signs, to ward off every evil except the ruin of time. Doors on three sides of the house opened on a wide gallery, so you could avoid the sun any time of day. But at a time of temporary prosperity, the roof over the gallery had been raised (you could still see the wound where the roof had been) and plantation-style columns installed in front of the house's main entrance. As the farm fell on hard times, more and more land was sold until all that remained was the present fifty acres, presided over by the imitation plantation manor.

The place was primitive beyond Reid's imagination. There is electric power now, but at that time the line stopped more than a mile from the house. The windows had to be propped open, and they were covered with cotton gauze in place of screens. The gauze filtered the sunlight and bellied in the softest breeze. There was an indoor toilet, but during dry spells, when the gravity feed from the springhouse was low, the privy behind the house was used.

Reid always knew that everyone in the family lied to keep up appearances, but Aunt Maddy and Uncle Walter worked it overtime. In any case, there was no need, not when it came to an object as beautiful as the huge cast-iron kitchen stove, with its double spring handles, its chrome trim around the cooking surface and chrome rail around the skirt. It was a relic from an age that was not long past in that part of Virginia. Aunt Maddy apologized for it to anyone who would listen.

Part of the fiction of Uncle Walter's squiredom was to have a handyman. Jimmy Lee Monk fit the part perfectly. He had lived in the area all his life, never advancing even to working shares. Past sixty, he had finally come to a safe berth. As long as the house didn't fall on their heads, the wood for the stove was chopped, and he looked like he was working, no one bothered him. "One foot on a ladder," he described himself, "the other in the grave." Every Friday afternoon he took off his overalls, shaved, put on a shiny serge suit no matter how hot it was, and walked to town. Monday morning he appeared with the Sunday Richmond *Times Leader* under his arm. He left the paper on the porch for Aunt Maddy, then disappeared into the converted tack room in the barn, which was his summer residence.

If Jimmy Lee was Uncle Walter's fiction, Wilma Banks was Aunt Maddy's. Wilma was the eldest child from a neighboring farm. She did the cleaning, the laundry, and the cooking because Aunt Maddy wanted nothing to do with that wood-burning behemoth in the kitchen.

By the end of the first week in the same house, Reid was in love with Wilma. Every time he heard her in the kitchen, laughing at something Jimmy Lee said, his jaw tightened and an echo of something that felt like loneliness overwhelmed him. She was five years his senior, so he knew the best he could hope for would be to be treated as a younger brother. But because of the nature of their relationship, he couldn't even hope for that. It never occurred to him that his situation was anything but hopeless. Anything other than hopeless was out of the question.

Wilma had broad shoulders, heavy breasts, short muscular arms, and long tapering legs. Her chin was a little longer than it should have been, but it was balanced with prominent cheekbones and soft blue eyes. She wore faded cotton dresses with squared necklines that showed the tops of her breasts. She went without shoes, except for walking the dusty road between her parents' farm and Aunt Maddy's place. Her hair, faded gold, almost white, was pinned at the back of her neck, but sometimes she wore it loose.

Reid's imagination was so taken with the possibilities of the loose hair, flowing softly like a sun-drenched stream, that he was encouraged to compliment her. She smiled down at him and curtsied, fingertips extending the hem of her dress. "Thank you kindly." Her teeth were white, but there was a gold filling near the gum line of her left eyetooth. Up close she gave off a female smell of violet perfume mixed with the odor of fresh sweat that Reid found exciting.

What he found most distracting about the girl was her invariable cheerfulness. He could never be sure she wasn't laughing at him, laughing at all of them, as though she was too proud of her humility to complain of Aunt Maddy's or Cousin Ashley's badgering. It was somehow all of a piece with what little Reid knew of her family.

Uncle Walter reported that he had offered the hay on the place to Wilma's father for what he thought it was worth. "I all but issued an invitation for him to cheat me," Uncle Walter said. "He took off that grimy engineer's cap he always wears and smiled at me. 'That's a mighty generous offer,' he says, 'and I thank you kindly. But I got all the hay I can use.' So I told him," Uncle Walter said, "'Look, Will, I don't know about farming, but I've been told that there's no such thing as having too much hay, as long as the price is right.'

"'I got all I can use,' he says."

Uncle Walter held up his hand as though he was still interrupting Will Banks. "'Wait a minute,' I told him. 'How does this sound? I'll give you the damned hay if you'll just cut it.'

"He slaps his cap on the side of his leg and shakes his head." Uncle Walter demonstrated each action.

"Maybe he expects you to pay him," Cousin Ashley said. His lips worked as though he wanted to smile but wasn't sure he was allowed.

"Hell will freeze three times over before I pay him to accept my hay," Uncle Walter said.

"Maybe he doesn't have the money," Reid said.

"I told him he could set his own price," Uncle Walter said. "Then I told him I'd give it to him."

Maybe he isn't the sort of person who can accept a gift if he thinks it's charity, Reid thought but kept his mouth shut.

Later he asked Jimmy Lee what he thought the hay was worth.

"You buying or selling?" Jimmy Lee asked.

"Neither."

"Then it ain't worth nothing." Jimmy Lee fished a penny nail from a paper sack and went back to fixing a loose sideboard at the base of the springhouse.

When it rained, Aunt Maddy, Cousin Ashley, and Reid played Scrabble most of the day. Cousin Ashley invented words. Aunt Maddy would laugh and let him get away with it. In good weather, Reid climbed the steep hill behind the house, until it flattened to a stand of walnut trees, then he climbed the shallow slope beyond to a grassy saddle between twin rounded peaks.

Sounds traveled beyond sight. He could hear Will Banks's cows tearing the grass from a pasture he couldn't see. Hear a voice shout from another world. Leaves from the walnut trees sounded like a summer storm. Yet within the sounds he was surrounded by a core of silence that even a hungry calf's bleating could not penetrate.

Every night after supper he crossed the dirt road to the barn whose roof had started to give way, then swung west through a pasture that ran parallel to the road Wilma would take on her way home. He walked as far as the squared wire fence, nailed to gray rotting posts that divided the two farms.

By the time Wilma passed he was almost blind from staring into the setting sun.

"Hey, Reid," she shouted. "See you in the morning."

He raised his arm but said nothing, because there was nothing worth saying. Nothing that wouldn't make him sound like a kid from the city who wasn't worth seeing the next morning, or any other morning.

Then one evening after a string of cloudless days, two things happened. The odds against their taking place simultaneously beyond calculation. Wilma hiked up her dress, climbed the wire squares of the fence, and jumped into the pasture. At the same time, two formless voices—a man's and a boy's—came at Reid directly out of the sunset.

"If that's the boyfriend," the boy's voice said, "he looks kind of puny."

Reid was short for his age and sensitive about it. He ate special foods and did exercises to increase his height. But he wasn't puny. If anything he was overweight. And sensitive about that too. If he thought anyone was looking at him, he would suck in his stomach and stick out his chest. With his red hair and thin face, it made him look like a stuffed bird.

Wilma laughed at the boy's comment, but that was her normal response to virtually everything.

"Minnie lost her calf and is about to bellow the barn down," the man's voice said. "You seen it anywhere?"

"No, sir," Wilma said. She grabbed Reid's arm and pulled him forward. "This is my daddy and my brother." Then to the figures who were still hidden in sunlight, "This here is Reid Stevenson the third. He's from Richmond, and he's real smart. He reads books all the time. Ask him anything."

A large hand came out of the sun. "Pleased to know you," the man said. His handshake was unexpectedly gentle.

"I'm Juney Banks," the boy said. "Juney Banks the first."

"That will do," the man said softly.

A dog yapped to Reid's left. They moved toward the noise, Will Banks and Juney purposefully, Wilma pulling Reid's arm as he moved in a dream, unsure whether he would wake and less sure if he wanted to.

Will and Juney cast long shadows as they walked ahead. The man's shadow thick as a mountain, motionless as the world seemed to roll around it. Juney's shadow, thin and spidery, skittering left and right to dodge the ancient piles of cow dung in the pockmarked field.

The sun dropped behind a hill and the air became thin and clear. Will stopped at a place where a pair of fence posts had rotted through and the wire was almost on the ground. He lifted his denim engineer's cap and wiped his forehead on the inside of his arm.

"You might mention to Mr. Snyder about them posts," he said to Wilma. "I'll fix them, but he ought to share the cost for wire if what there is won't do."

Juney ran ahead, toward the noise of the barking dog. Reid knew a Blair in school. And there was an Evelyn on the football team. But he had never known a Juney. Suddenly it came to him that Juney stood for Junior, and he felt embarrassed not to have figured it out immediately.

They found the calf curled around itself. A shaggy black and white dog barked and danced, daring the calf to move. Juney held the dog while Will Banks lifted the calf in both arms and carried it up a hill toward his barn. As soon as Juney released the dog it jumped around Will's feet.

"Get that fool dog out from under me before I tromple him," he said.

Juney lunged for the dog, which scooted away and resumed barking in a widening circle.

At the entrance to the Banks's barn Reid stopped, overcome by the acid stench of manure and soured milk. In the dim light he could see Will carry the calf into a box stall while Juney watched. Then Juney turned, lifted his straw hat, and wiped his forehead as his father had done. His hair was dark and cut so close that Reid could make out the pale skin of his scalp.

"How old are you?" Juney asked.

"I'll be fourteen."

Juney laughed. "I'll be seventy-seven. If I live that long." He clapped his hat back on his head, then pushed it down until it made his ears stand out. "You want to go fishing?"

"When?"

"Now. Tonight. Ever catch eels?"

"Lots of times," Reid lied.

"Can Reid go eeling with us, Pa?"

"That damn calf peed all over me when we was coming up the hill," Will said from the doorway of the barn.

"I thought you was walking kind of funny," Juney said.

"You'd walk funny too if you had calf pee running down your arm and onto your leg."

"Can Reid go eeling with us?" Juney asked again.

"I don't see why not. If it's all right with his folks."

They started walking toward the house, Will between the two boys, an arm around each of them. Reid could not help wondering whether he had the clean arm or the other.

"He says he fished for eels before," Juney said.

Reid shook his head in the sudden darkness. "I didn't say eels," he insisted. "I don't know anything about eels. Aren't there some that if you grab their tails they shock you?"

"Not if you put salt on them," Will said.

Juney detached himself from his father, picked up a stone, and skated it across a pond. "We got trout in there as big as your arm," he said.

As they came to the house Will released Reid's shoulder. "Watch that step," Will said. "It's a little tricky until you get used to it."

A two-inch board was set on a pair of rounded stones. It tipped back when Reid stepped on it, then suddenly forward, throwing him against the doorjamb.

"I keep meaning to fix it," Will said, "as soon as I get the time."

The house was dark and small, made smaller by the cracked ceiling tiles, whose corners were raw and peeling, and by the thick smell of ancient grease. But there was so little furniture the house seemed almost empty. A tufted horsehair sofa with tilted arms, a wooden rocker, two straight chairs with torn cane seats. The floor was covered by a sheet of faded red and green linoleum. Red and green flowered wallpaper, also faded, was decorated with framed photographs of what Reid assumed were family members.

"This here is Reid Stevenson the third," Wilma said. She had gone to the house when the others went to the barn. The sound of her voice made Reid realize he hadn't missed her.

"Pleased to meet you, Reid, I'm sure," an old woman said. She had a sharp hollow face with coarse skin, seamed and cracked. Black hair escaped as it stretched across her head to a tight bun. Her front teeth were packed together, but tipped at different angles. Behind them an occasional tooth stood lonely as a sentinel. A black dress hung unevenly and bagged across her flat chest. A greasy piece of muslin tucked around her waist served as an apron. "Wilma's told us about how smart you are, reading all them books."

"He's going eeling with us," Juney said.

"Can I go too, Ma?" Wilma asked.

The idea that the old woman was Wilma's mother was something Reid had never considered.

"They's some things I need for you to help me with."

"I'll do them tomorrow. I promise," Wilma said.

"At least feed the baby," Mrs. Banks said.

As if on cue, a baby wailed from somewhere up a narrow flight of stairs.

"Go ahead," Will said. "I got to change my shirt and put on fresh overalls."

Reid and Juney waited outside, in the dark.

"What grade you in?" Juney asked.

"Ninth."

"Me too."

That seemed hardly possible to Reid. Juney stood a good head taller, and even in the dim lamplight in the house Reid had seen the shadow of hair on Juney's upper lip.

They were joined by a younger boy, whom Juney introduced as Randall. His hair was even shorter than his brother's. Mrs. Banks's voice came through the gauze-covered window. "Junius, you take your brother with you."

"Junius?" Reid couldn't help saying.

"Ain't it a pistol?" Juney laughed. "It was my grandpa's name."

"And you look just like him," Randall piped.

"What do you know about it?" Juney demanded. "He was dead before you was born."

"Ma says—"

"Ma says," Juney mocked. "All you know is Ma says."

Will came out of the house, followed by Wilma. They each rocked expertly on the front step. "Let's go," Will said.

Everyone piled into an ancient Studebaker that reeked of oil and manure, the boys in back, Wilma beside her father in front. Will turned on the ignition, released the hand brake, and let the car coast downhill. "Starter's busted," he explained as he threw the car into gear. It jerked and the engine caught. "Got to remember to always park on a hill."

"Or carry enough passengers to push," Wilma added.

The car slowed and Randall wanted to know why they were stopping.

"So Reid can tell his people where he's going," Will said.

Cousin Ashley wasn't around, which was good because he might have asked to be included. Not that he would want to go anywhere with the Banks family but just to spoil things for Reid. There was a light coming from Aunt Maddy's room. Reid tapped at the door and waited.

"Is that you, Reid?"

"Yes, ma'am." Then mumbling the words together so they couldn't be understood, "IsitallrightifIgofishingwiththe-Banks?" And waited for the answer he knew would follow.

"That's nice, dear."

At the river, flashlights and kerosene lanterns seemed to light the sounds of splashing and laughter. There were more than a dozen men and women. Reid eased his way toward the river-bank to learn how to catch an eel when Juney shoved a bottle of something into Reid's hand.

"You drink beer?" Juney asked.

"Sure," Reid lied.

"Honest?"

"Scout's oath." Since Reid had never been a scout of any kind, it took the edge off the lie.

Randall wanted some too, but Juney wouldn't let him have it.

"I'll tell Ma you was drinking again," Randall threatened.

"You do, and I'll bust your head so hard you'll be whistling through your belly button."

Reid thought he saw Wilma standing in the water up to her knees, with her skirt tucked in her belt. She bent forward and he thought he could see her underpants.

Juney led Reid away, so the two of them could drink in private. After the second beer, Reid didn't even try to keep up. Juney passed him the bottle. Reid raised it to his closed lips and handed it back to Juney.

"Pa says if it don't rain we're going to start the second haying tomorrow," Juney said.

Reid nodded as though he had thought it over and decided tomorrow was as good a time as any.

"It's damned hard work," Juney added, "but it's kind of fun too."

Reid tried to concentrate on the words, as though he was translating from a foreign language. "Do you think it would be all right if I came and watched?"

"Last year we had Wilma," Juney said. "But with her working for your aunt, all we got is Randall. And you can guess how much help he is."

"Maybe I could help," Reid suggested. He had never done any real work, and the idea of it caught his imagination.

"You ever hayed?"

"Sure," Reid lied.

"This ain't like most haying," Juney said. "We ain't got a tractor to do the mowing."

"That's all right," Reid said.

"Pa keeps saying we'll get one, but he never does." Juney offered Reid the last of the beer. Reid held up his hand, and

Juney tipped the bottle back and emptied it, then threw the bottle as far as he could into the river.

"Do you think he'll let me help?" Reid asked.

"I don't know," Juney said. "It ain't just hard work, it's dangerous."

"You could ask him," Reid suggested.

"You ought to see our horses," Juney laughed. "They look like they're ready for the glue factory."

Reid laughed too because he didn't want to offend Juney. "When are you going to ask?"

"Ask what?"

"Your dad about me helping with the haying," Reid said.

"Time enough in the morning."

"You want to see what they're doing at the river?" Reid said. They could run into Will and Juney could ask him. It wouldn't be likely Will would turn Reid down right to his face.

"They ain't doing nothing but splashing theirselves," Juney said.

The next thing Reid knew was the car jolting him awake, then its motion lulling him back to sleep. When the car stopped he stumbled out and started up the steep drive before he remembered to thank Will for taking him.

"We was going anyway," Will said.

The car started to pull away when Juney leaned out the window and shouted, "See you in the morning."

Reid made it to the room he shared with Cousin Ashley without waking anyone, undressed, and fell in bed. He tried to remember why he would see Juney in the morning. Then he concentrated on Wilma's backside, with her dress up and her underpants showing.

When he came into the kitchen the next morning, Wilma was shelling peas, a large metal pan gripped between her thighs. She put the pan on the table when she saw Reid, stood, and brushed the front of her skirt. "Pa says it's all right."

He wondered what was all right but not enough to ask.

"Juney shouldn't have give you that beer," she said. "If Ma

ever finds out she'll kill him." She threw wood in the iron stove's belly and broke two eggs in a skillet. "You eat something and you'll feel better. That's what Pa always does." The yolks ran as she tried to flip the eggs. "They's biscuits and side meat." She pulled a platter from the warming oven, using her apron to keep from burning her fingers. "You going to need your strength if you help with the haying."

That was what was all right, what Reid had been trying to remember. He was more pleased than if he had won an unexpected prize but unwilling to show his pleasure.

Wilma slid the eggs to a plate and put them in front of Reid. "They'll be in the north field. That's where they always start. You know where that is?" Reid nodded but she wasn't watching him. "You go to the barn, then follow the ruts to the left up a rise. You'll hear the mower and Pa yelling."

Aunt Maddy sat on the front porch, working one of her crossword puzzles. "Where are you off to?" she asked.

"Mr. Banks asked me to help him with his haying."

"That's nice," Aunt Maddy said. "You have a good time. And be careful."

It hadn't rained for more than a week and Reid's feet raised gritty puffs of red dust. At the crest of a hill he looked back and saw Aunt Maddy on the porch. Wilma came halfway out the door, said something, then disappeared back into the house.

Reid found the ruts beside the barn and followed them until he could look down on Will Banks, sitting in a contraption hitched behind a pair of horses. The horses saw Reid first and stopped. Will shook their reins without looking up. "What the Sam Hill—" He finally glanced up and saw Reid.

Juney and Randall stood panting beside the horses. The boys were stripped to the waist, their hard bodies covered with streams of dust, flecked with stipples of fresh-cut grass.

"We was wondering when you was going to show up," Juney said. "An hour more and you could be on time for lunch."

"Give this man your fork, Randall, and get yourself another," Will said.

Randall leaped at the suggestion. He let his pitchfork drop into Reid's hand and was off across the meadow.

"You be back in five minutes," Will yelled at Randall, who raised an arm without breaking stride. "All right," Will said, "we got us a job of work to do."

The horses jerked forward and Reid watched the blades of the mower slide back and forth. They made a clacking sound that was loud at first but quickly blended into the other sounds of the day.

Juney pitched the cut grass out of the row and behind the track of the horses and mower. Reid took his place beside Juney and tried to imitate his actions.

Instead of turning back in the same direction he had come, Will cut a shorter row at the end of the field and started a fresh row. The two boys raced behind, swinging their pitchforks with each stride to get the grass out of the way of the next pass.

"Take off your shirt," Juney gasped.

Reid undid the buttons, then hesitated. If he removed the shirt he would have to hold in his stomach, and he wasn't sure he could manage it all morning. He glanced at how far ahead the mower was, threw off the shirt, and raced to catch up.

They worked across the top of the field and started down the other side. At the end of each row, Will reined the horses, and waited for the boys.

"You getting the hang of it," he said to Reid. "Swing easy and keep moving. Nothing to it."

At every third or fourth swing, instead of catching the grass Reid dug his pitchfork into the ground, jolting his shoulders and making his hands sting as the tines complained. Juney glanced back from time to time but said nothing. Will pretended not to notice. Reid's arms ached and he could feel the start of blisters each time the pitchfork slid through his fingers.

The pauses at the end of each row became longer as Will waited for Reid, panting and sweating, to catch up. But as soon as he arrived, Will moved on. Reid's anger at Will multiplied. It lodged in Reid's throat and made it hard for him to swallow. He raised a forearm to wipe the sweat from his face and caught the tears that hung dangerously in the corners of his eyes. Will ought to have some consideration that Reid had offered to help, not do the whole job himself. And Will should make some allowance for the fact that this was Reid's first attempt at haying.

The runs across the top and bottom of the field were abandoned, and Will moved up one side and down the other. The boys had to work faster, and Reid swore solemnly that if God would let him survive the morning he would never come here again.

Then suddenly the mower moved through the final row. Juney threw himself on the ground in the partial shade of the elephant-ear leaves of a catalpa. Reid walked slowly, afraid that if he moved too fast his knees would buckle.

"Rest while you can," Juney said.

"I'm all right," Reid answered. He planted his pitchfork and leaned against it.

Will raised the mower blade and drove the team to the fence gate. "I told you five minutes," he yelled.

Randall appeared at the other side of the fence, a wicker basket held chest high. "Ma made me wait while she fixed sandwiches."

Will tied off the reins, jumped down from the mower, and took the basket. He set it on the ground and squatted beside it. "Let's see your hand," he said to Reid.

Reid leaned over him until their heads were at the same level. Will's thumbs stroked the palms, poking gently and watching the boy's face. "Couple of days they'll be tough as hide," he said.

But Reid had already decided that in less time than that the whole morning would be a distant memory.

"They sore?" Juney asked.

Reid shook his head.

"Let's see what Ma fixed," Will said. He held up a sandwich to the sun. "Lookee here. Peanut butter. Now, ain't that a surprise? We ain't had peanut butter since yesterday."

They ate the sandwiches without talking, then stretched out

and stared into the endless sky. Reid could see that the universe was curved, but he didn't dare announce his observation. Juney probably would laugh, and Will would pretend he didn't hear. Anything to avoid Reid's lecture about what neither of them could understand.

"You know what we been cutting?" Will asked.

Reid sat up and shook his head. "No, sir." He felt awkward saying sir to Will but knew it would have felt more awkward not to.

Without rising, Will reached for a handful of grass and offered it to Reid. "That's fescue. Meadow fescue. The part that ain't weed."

"We got alfalfa too," Juney said.

"And not enough of either to get us through a hard winter," Will added.

Reid made a note of the information, not sure what he should do about it. He had been right about Will Banks not accepting what he thought was charity, but being right seemed less important than that there be enough hay to get them through the winter.

In the distance Reid heard Randall yelling at the horses. The air was so still that his high-pitched voice seemed to come from another county.

Will, Juney, and Reid rose and followed the sound. Juney closed the gate behind them, picking up the end that trailed the ground and carrying it in her arm, then hooking it shut with a length of chain.

Will arrived at the mower first and reached over a wheel for the bucket of water that sloshed between Randall's feet. He held the dipper in his fist, tipped his head back, and drank. Then he offered the water to Reid. The boy drank with his head back, as Will had done, but half the water slid past his chin, over his chest, and into his khaki pants, where it ran down one leg in an irregular stain.

Juney laughed, grabbed the dipper, and used it to point at Reid's pants. Reid looked down and smiled at his own misfortune.

As soon as Will unhooked the chain from the gate of an uncut field of fescue, the end of the gate sagged to the ground. Reid grabbed it, as Juney had done, and swung it open.

"We forgot the damn lunch basket," Will said to Randall. "Run over and carry it back to the house." Randall jumped from the mower and started back to the cut field. "And be back here by the time I count one hundred," Will added.

"That's the last we see of him today," Juney said and threw the dipper back in the bucket.

Reid remembered that he had meant to leave, but he didn't see how he could, not after eating the Bankses' food, and knowing how undependable Randall was.

After two hours of steady work, they rested. Then Juney took his father's place on the mower.

Reid worked easier beside Will than he had with Juney. Will swung his fork in a long arc, as though he meant to cut the grass and not merely throw it out of the way. Reid tried to imitate the motion and found that he dug his fork into the ground less often. Let others lead, he was perfectly willing to follow.

When they stopped, part of the field was still uncut. Will drove the mower through the gate and waited while Juney closed it. Then Juney moved beside the horses and laced his fingers together, palms up. "Give you a boost," he said to Reid.

One hundred yards from the barn, Juney and then Reid slid from the horses' backs. Juney headed down a wagon track with Reid beside him toward the herd of cows grazing a hillside pasture.

"You oughtn't to suck in your gut," Juney said as soon as they were alone. "It got to interfere with your breathing. Pa says a person's lungs should have nothing to construct them."

Reid let his stomach out slowly, a fraction of an inch at each breath.

"You ain't fat anyway," Juney added. "Kind of chubby, but not fat."

Will, Mrs. Banks, and Randall were waiting to begin milking by the time Juney and Reid brought the cows to the barn.

After milking, everyone walked to the house. Reid knew he

should be heading home, but he was unable to break the connection. He sat on the baked ground in front of the house with Juney and Randall. Inside the house a baby cried. A thick odor of cooking came through the open window. Will sat smoking a pipe, rocking in and out of view.

"I got to get home," Reid said but made no move to rise.

"You coming tomorrow?" Will said through the window.

"If you want me."

"Sure we want you," Will said, then rocked out of view.

Reid walked home with the sun at his back and with the sure knowledge that for at least one more day there was a place for him to be. Halfway up the drive he heard Cousin Ashley's laugh. Then Aunt Maddy's voice, as severe as it would ever get. "Where were you? We've been waiting supper thirty minutes. I wouldn't be surprised if everything isn't ruined."

"I was at the Bankses'. I told you I was going," Reid said. Then to Cousin Ashley, "What's so funny?"

"You," he said but stopped laughing.

"I didn't know you meant all day," Aunt Maddy said. "What in the world could you find to do?" Then without waiting for an answer, "You look like you've been rolling in dirt. Wash up and put on a shirt, so we can eat." Reid crossed the porch and had his hand on the doorknob. "Just a minute, young man." Aunt Maddy stood and pointed at Reid's bare chest. "Where is your shirt? I distinctly remember you were wearing one this morning."

"I must have forgot it," Reid said.

"Forgotten," Cousin Ashley corrected.

"Forgot it indeed," Aunt Maddy said. "That was an expensive shirt. You can just turn right around and go back and find it." Reid started to do as she told him. "Not now," she said. "Supper is already late. You can do it after we eat."

"It will be dark then," Reid said.

"Then do it tomorrow. And don't think I'll forget."

Cousin Ashley stood behind his mother. He raised one eyebrow and shook his head. Reid tried not to smile.

"I fail to see anything the least bit humorous," Aunt Maddy

said. "I think someone your age could show a little consideration."

"Yes, ma'am," Reid agreed, and retreated into the house.

After he washed and put on a clean shirt, he cut through the kitchen to get to the dining room.

"Looks like you survived all right," Wilma said. "How are your hands?"

"They're fine," Reid said.

"The first day in the field my hands always hurt something awful. And I'm used to it. I guess boys is tougher than girls."

"I guess so," Reid agreed and hurried into the dining room.

The next morning he was out of bed and dressed before Wilma arrived. He met Jimmy Lee in the kitchen, where the old man was fixing his breakfast.

"You're up mighty early," Jimmy Lee said.

"Couldn't sleep," Reid answered, for some reason unwilling to confess why he was anxious for the day to start.

"Heard you was helping Will Banks with his haying."

Reid flushed and nodded. He wanted to tell Jimmy Lee about it but was afraid the old man would laugh or patronize him.

"Bad for a man to be out in the hot sun all day withouten a hat. Could give a person sunstroke." Jimmy Lee pushed the enamel coffee pot off the hot part of the stove. "I got this old straw I could let you use, if you've a mind to."

"I'd be much obliged," Reid said softly, so as not to betray his excitement. "But I wouldn't want to deprive you."

"I won't be working in the sun for a while." If Jimmy Lee noticed the boy's excitement, or his shift to a country accent, he gave no sign. "You watch that the coffee don't boil over, I'll get it."

It took a pair of folds of last Sunday's *Times Leader* under the sweatband to make the hat fit and it was still a little big as Reid examined himself in the hall mirror, twisting his head as far as he could, trying to see how he looked from the back and sides. Then he returned to the kitchen, where Jimmy Lee was scrambling eggs in bacon grease. "You sure it's all right?"

Jimmy Lee squinted into the thick smoke. "I ain't giving it to you. And I'll thank you to take care and see it don't get lost."

The second day's work was like the first. They finished mowing the field they had left partially cut, then moved on to the next. The weather was unchanged, a hot baking sun, cloudless sky heavy with heat. Reid felt different about the work and about himself and he was grateful that no one seemed to notice. They didn't even mention Jimmy Lee's hat, which in spite of the folded newspaper in the sweatband tended to slide over Reid's forehead. When they broke for lunch, Reid remembered to pick up the shirt he had forgotten the previous day.

He tried to think what it would be like to have Will for a father, Juney and Randall for brothers, and Wilma for a sister. Reid knew the idea wouldn't fit even before he tried it on, but the thought was so attractive that he held it long after it had stopped making sense and put it aside a little at a time. In the end all he could cling to was the work. He was doing a job that needed doing. It would get done without him, but that did not mean he wasn't needed. Being needed was the irreducible element that he could not surrender.

They worked through that day and another before the mowing was completed. Throughout the final day Reid felt a sense of loss with each swing of his pitchfork. The end of a row was like the sight of a door slowly closing.

"I guess haying is over," he said to Juney as they walked back to the barn behind the herd of cows.

"Mowing's the easy part. Now comes the work." Juney stopped and threw a stone at the bull. "The hay don't march into the barn. We got to carry it there. And we ain't even got a baler." He threw another stone at the bull, who had moved out of range. "Pa bought one used, but it broke and he can't fix it." He kicked a dried cow turd with the toe of his boot. "It's just like every other damn thing we got. We buy it secondhand, it breaks, and if Pa can't fix it, then it stays broke. Someday I swear I'm going to buy something brand new with a guarantee. And when it don't work I'm going to take it back to the dealer and tell him to fix it."

The next day they began raking and stacking the dried fescue. Juney was right about the work. In place of the mower, Will rode in front of the huge parabolic steel teeth of the hay rake, which stroked the ground, gathering the hay until the semicircle was filled. Will raised the teeth with a metal lever, moved forward a few feet, then lowered the teeth and began again. Juney, Reid, and even Randall ran to the hay Will had left, split it into armfuls, gathered the stragglers, and stood the hay on end, filling the field with thatched roofs for a leprechaun settlement. Dust caked the boys' faces. The dried beards of fescue found their way into the boys' eyes and nose. When they finally rested, Reid could taste the hay and continued to taste it even after he had repeatedly rinsed his mouth from the bucket of water that was kept against one fence.

By the time the field was cleared and the wagon was piled high, the hay seemed to sway in the faint breeze that came late each afternoon. Will climbed over the front hub and took the reins from Randall. Juney reached down and pulled Reid onto the wagon, where the two boys lay, swaying and jouncing over the rutted track, stubble biting their bare backs. In the western sky Reid noticed a small cloud, the first one he had seen for more than a week.

Raking the hay, stacking it, then bringing it in and getting it into the barn became the pattern of Reid's days. It took almost as long to unload the wagon as it took to load it. One day they would load the wagon twice and unload it once before it was time for milking. The next day they started with unloading, picked up the next load, then brought it to the barn.

It hadn't rained for two weeks, but the small cloud Reid had seen in the west multiplied every day. Sooner or later the rain would come, and it would be that much harder for every day it delayed.

"That's the way it is," Will said. "Every farmer who ever lived had to race the weather." But it didn't make Will change his pace.

"At least we could work on Sunday," Reid suggested.

"That's the Lord's day."

"But you don't go to church," Reid insisted. "And even if you did, there's half a day left."

"The Bible says God worked six days and rested on the seventh," Will said, his tone getting harsher as Reid seemed unable to drop the issue.

"If it rains and the hay is ruined—"

"What God does to my hay is His business," Will snapped. "What I do is mine. What I don't need is folks telling me how to run my life."

Reid felt his own anger rise to answer Will's. "That doesn't make any sense. You know you can't afford to lose the hay. And if it means—"

Will's jaw set. "If'n you don't like the way I do things, then you can take yourself out of here and work for someone else." He pointed down the road. "That ends it," he added.

Later, Juney waited until his father drove the hay rake beyond hearing. "You're right," he whispered to Reid. "And that old man knows it. He's just too damned stubborn to admit when he's wrong. Like he won't buy a milking machine no matter how many times I tell him." Reid nodded and continued working. "Don't worry that he yells at you," Juney said. "He yells at all of us."

Reid nodded again, unable to tell Juney that being yelled at by Will was as though a cactus, full of spikes, had produced a delicate flower.

The following day the wind shifted to the east. "Looks like we're going to get your rain," Will said to Reid.

"Can we get the rest of the hay in before it hits?"

"Maybe." Will spoke so slowly it sounded like two words. "At least it will make Ma happy to get some water on her garden."

Reid was not interested in the benefits the rain would bring. "It looks to me," he said, "that we have four wagonloads."

"Three, if we overload," Will said.

"Three or four, we better get going. That rain won't wait forever." Not even Will seemed to question Reid's authority.

"And that's a fact," Will said. Then to Randall, "Tell your ma we need her to drive the wagon. She can bring the baby with her. And get your tail right back here," he added. "This time I ain't fooling. We got us a job of work to do."

The rain began as they were putting the last load on the wagon. A mist at first, then needle points that stood like beads before running down their bodies. Will threw his pitchfork and jumped onto the wagon in one motion. He took the reins from his wife and clicked at the horses until they broke into a trot. Juney reached down and pulled Reid aboard. The two boys lay on their stomachs, legs braced against the wagon stakes, as the top-heavy wagon jounced over deep ruts. Randall tried to run beside the wagon, falling further and further behind.

Will drove right into the barn. It was raining hard by the time Randall reached them.

"We done it," he yelled.

His voice was the signal for everyone to come back to motion. Will jumped to the barn floor, then took the baby while his wife climbed down. Juney and Reid slid down the hay and brushed the dust from their chests. Reid removed his hat and mopped his forehead with the inside of his arm.

"A good job of work," Will said. "A damn good job of work."

The baby began to hiccup, then cry. Mrs. Banks bounced the child gently in her arms.

"I'll be going to town in the morning to pick up some things," Will said to Reid. "You come by before milking tomorrow and I'll have your wage."

If Reid had not been so surprised by the offer, he might have protested. Then he was glad he hadn't. Of course he had not been working with the expectation of being paid, but that did not mean he couldn't be proud that someone actually considered his labor valuable enough to deserve to be rewarded.

He moved to the barn door, grunted, and nodded to the rain. As soon as he was sure of his voice he turned. "Guess I better head home," he managed to say before his throat closed down again.

"Thank you, Reid," Mrs. Banks said. "I don't know what we would have done without you."

"Amen." Will nodded.

Reid started to answer, then realized he couldn't. He raised a hand to eye level, used it to pull his hat over his eyes, threw his shirt over his shoulder, and stepped into the rain. He walked slowly, allowing himself to enjoy his triumph. Even with the hat tipped low, the rain blew into his face and ran down his cheeks like tears.

By the time he reached home, his mind had raced ahead to what he would do with the money. Buy something showy, he decided immediately. Something that his friends would have to notice. They would ask him where he got it, and he would explain that he bought it with the money he earned working on a farm during the summer.

He yearned for his younger days when his teacher would invariably ask the class to write essays on how they had spent their summer. Now that he had something important to tell it was unlikely anyone would ask, unless he forced the issue.

He sat on the edge of the porch, considering what he should buy. Of course, it depended on how much Will paid him. But if it wasn't enough for something really impressive, he could add to the wage from his savings. If he didn't tell, no one would be the wiser.

He watched the heifers Uncle Walter had imported from another farm try to get out of the rain and into the barn. Jimmy Lee was yelling at them, but they crowded under the ruined eaves.

"You're drenched," Aunt Maddy said. Reid turned to see her framed by the doorway. "The idea, sitting in the rain without even a shirt."

"I'm all right," Reid said.

"I want you to take a hot bath this instant. Then put on dry clothes."

"I'm all right," Reid repeated.

Dinner was late. With all the dry weather, Wilma had taken to leaving the tinder box uncovered, so when it finally rained all her kindling got wet and she had a time getting the big iron stove to stay lit. Late dinner always made Aunt Maddy cranky.

Cousin Ashley had a head start as far as crankiness was concerned. Seeing Reid so full of himself did nothing to ease the situation.

Reid knew he shouldn't say anything, that they wouldn't understand, but the words formed themselves so clearly that he could taste their shape. He held back until they were all seated at the table and the kerosene lamp that hung on a pulley had been pulled down, lit, then pushed back in place.

"The haying's over," he said, still not sure how much he was willing to share.

"That's nice, dear," Aunt Maddy said.

The rain had stopped and the wind died. The air had a sodden quality. Wilma had deep circles of sweat under her arms and across her back when she brought dinner to the table.

"At least we can stop worrying that you'll kill yourself," Cousin Ashley said. "And poor Will Banks can get some work done." He turned to his mother. "How much did you pay him to let Reid hang around there?"

"Stop teasing your cousin," Aunt Maddy smiled.

Wilma brought a platter of gray meat that looked as though whatever animal it had once been had died of anemia.

"What in the name of God is that?" Cousin Ashley said.

"The danged stove is acting funny," Wilma said. Hair stuck to her forehead and the sides of her face. She tried to brush it aside but it wouldn't move.

Cousin Ashley waited until she had returned to the kitchen, then said in a voice loud enough for her to hear, "I don't think it's the danged stove, I think it's the danged cook that's acting up."

As Aunt Maddy tried to carve the meat, the knife slipped from the surface and banged against the platter. "I wonder what it was," she mused.

"Dinosaur?" Cousin Ashley suggested.

Reid caught himself smiling and was ashamed. He was taking the wrong side, against Wilma, against the Bankses, and lining up with Cousin Ashley. "It isn't Wilma's fault," he said.

"It isn't the dinosaur's," Cousin Ashley laughed.

Aunt Maddy continued to try to carve. This time the meat slid from the platter and landed on the tablecloth. She speared it with her fork and returned it to the platter.

"I think we should drive a stake through it and bury it," Cousin Ashley said.

Aunt Maddy sat and studied the roast as though considering her son's suggestion. She held the carving knife and fork straight up in either hand.

It was then that Reid decided he had to speak. To defend himself. Or defend the Bankses. Or at least make it clear where he stood. "Will told me to come back tomorrow to pick up my wage." He was sorry the moment he said it. Ashamed of himself. It wasn't what he had meant to say, except the more he thought of it, the more he had to admit it was exactly what he meant. It did nothing to show that he was lined up with the Bankses against his own family. At best he seemed to be in a middle position.

Cousin Ashley laughed so hard he had to wipe his eyes with his napkin. Aunt Maddy looked concerned.

"That was very nice of Mr. Banks," she said. "And I don't think you should call him Will."

"Everybody calls him Will," Reid said.

"I don't," Aunt Maddy answered. "But that isn't what I meant."

"Reid Stevenson the third, Will Banks's hired man," Cousin Ashley said. "At least he offered you money. He could have offered you shares and you wouldn't have gotten anything."

"There's nothing humorous about it," Aunt Maddy snapped. She used the carving knife as a pointer. "The Bankses are a very poor family. Mr. Banks is a very unsuccessful farmer. I understand there are times when they don't have enough to eat."

"We could offer them our dinner," Cousin Ashley said.

"That's enough, young man," Aunt Maddy said, then turned back to Reid. "You don't take money from people like that."

Reid started to say something, but she held up the knife.

"I understand there are days when the Banks children go

hungry, when the only food they get is what is handed out free at school." She patted the roast with the side of the knife, then pointed to the kitchen. "Why do you think I keep that girl?" Her voice was loud enough for Wilma to hear every word. "She can't clean because no one ever showed her how. And God knows she can't cook."

"But what will Mr. Banks think if I don't show up?" Reid asked.

"He'll be relieved," Cousin Ashley muttered.

"There's a thing called noblesse oblige," Aunt Maddy said. "And you're never too young to learn it. I'm sure that when Mr. Banks thinks about it he'll understand exactly what I'm talking about."

After what was left of dinner, Reid went to the kitchen. Wilma was sitting at the white enamel table, her head propped in her hands. She glanced at him as he entered, then roughed her eyes with the heels of her hands.

"I'm sorry," he said and realized that if he could apologize for his aunt and cousin it proved beyond doubt that they were a part of his family, no matter how different he thought himself.

"I hate all of you," she said, as if to prove his point. "You're all so goddamned high and mighty."

"Why don't you quit?" he asked.

"Don't you think I want to?" She dropped her hands to her lap and stared at them. "I get half again as much working here as I could get anyplace else. And I don't have to spend nothing to get here."

"What do you think I should do?" Reid asked.

Wilma ignored the question. "Your aunt's right. People like her are always right. I do the best I can, but it ain't good enough for her because nothing is ever good enough for them kind of people."

"I think you do fine," he said gallantly.

"You don't know nothing about it. You mean well, but you're just a kid."

He turned to leave.

"You got no right asking me what you should do," she called after him. "There's things you got to decide for yourself."

He had already decided. And knew that he was making the wrong choice. But the right choice was too difficult. It was easier to be wrong for reasons people could believe than to be right for reasons they could not accept.

The next morning he took a book, headed for the hill beyond the house, and settled into the swale beyond the grove of walnut trees. He tried to tell himself that he and Will were even. There had been a debt on one side, and now there was a debt on the other. By refusing to collect what was owed him, Reid erased what he owed. But he knew he could never explain something like that to Will. Without meaning to, he had forced Will to accept a charity, and Reid knew Will would never forgive him.

Reid heard Juney yelling at Randall, then Will's voice yelling at both Randall and Juney.

The following day Reid returned the straw hat to Jimmy Lee.

"Keep it," Jimmy Lee said. "You got it broke in for your head now."

THE STRADIVARIUS

Thirty years ago there were plenty of places like Minks Mill in the Virginia mountains. They weren't on any map, and folks said there was no way to find them except by accident. But you could just as easily have said the only way to find them was to know exactly where you were going, because it was no accident that brought Jesse McCord there. He not only found Minks Mill but knew Boone Eliot was the man to see.

Boone heard the way the engine of the blue De Soto was missing long before he saw McCord pull into the yard and stop below the springhouse. Boone figured whoever it was had come to him to get his car straightened out. People were always doing that because if it had wheels Boone could fix it.

McCord took his time getting out of the car, then draped himself on the open door and leaned around the windshield. "Eliot?" he said. "Boone Eliot, the musician?"

There was nothing that could have given Boone more pleasure than to hear himself referred to as a musician instead of a car mechanic. He nodded, then leaned over and spat onto the moss that grew like a green bib from the lattice beneath the porch. "You a musician?"

"Does a goat stink?" McCord slammed the car door. He had bushy blond hair, a fox face with a long chin, and a moustache that wasn't much more than a golden line across his lip. His blue shirt was buttoned to the neck and the sleeves rolled down in spite of the heat of the late May afternoon. He looked to be about fifty, but it was hard to tell.

"What do you play?" Boone asked.

"Anything that needs it." McCord reached into the car and

pulled the key from the ignition. "But mostly fiddle." He had a pleasant voice with an accent Boone couldn't place.

Boone stood and his thick square face disappeared into shadow, reappearing in sunlight as he came halfway down the porch steps. He was a big man, six foot four or five and weighed close to two hundred and fifty but bulky more than fat. Ordinarily he never moved until whoever came to see him stated his business, but this man, whatever his name, had more right answers than Boone had questions.

Boone waited on the step for the stranger to come around the car. When the man still didn't move, Boone descended the remaining steps, crossed the yard, and stepped over the spring that appeared at the base of the hill above the house.

Finally the man shook himself free and stuck out his hand. "Jesse McCord," he said. "From east Tennessee."

That explained the peculiar accent. "The car giving you trouble?" Boone asked. It had to be the engine missing and all the musician talk was just to loosen Boone up, because as good as he was, everybody knew if he didn't feel like working on a man's car there was nothing could make him. But he was always ready for music. He would go as far as two hundred miles to play and almost as far just to listen. Someone must have told McCord the way Boone felt, especially about the fiddle, and the stranger was trying to butter him up.

"I can talk about cars to any damned fool," McCord said. "Got something I want to show you."

Boone had already popped the hood and was leaning over the engine. "Here it is. You got a loose wire from your number three to the distributor."

"To hell with my number three."

Boone was suddenly suspicious. If McCord hadn't found him to have his car fixed, then he had to be selling something.

McCord bounced the car keys in the palm of his hand as he walked toward the back of the car. He was a short stringy fellow and seemed to skate along the ground.

"You a salesman?" Boone asked.

"Not exactly." He opened the trunk and pulled out a shiny leatherette violin case. "Used to sell all kind of things. Bibles, The Home Encyclopedia of Medical Knowledge, lightning rods, sewing machines. Even sold silos for a time and all sort of farm machinery." He polished the leatherette case with his sleeve. "You name it I sold it one time or another."

"I knew it," Boone started to say, but McCord cut him off just the way a salesman would.

"The Home Encyclopedia was best. No telling how many lives I saved with that book." He held the case by its handle. "Is there someplace we can get out of the sun?"

For a "not exactly" salesman Boone thought McCord was making a pretty good pitch. "Come up on the porch," he said and led the way. "Mind the spring."

A dumpy woman with thick thighs and a heavy bosom came around the corner of the house. She wore a large straw hat with a pull string under her chin and faded men's overalls that looked as if they had shrunk while she had grown to fill them to capacity. "I heard voices," she started to say, then saw the stranger and tried to back out of sight. "I didn't know—"

"This here is Mr. McCord," Boone said. "Mr. Jesse McCord all the way from east Tennessee." It had a ring to it and Boone smiled.

"Pleased to meet you, ma'am," McCord said.

"My wife Molly," Boone said.

"Don't look at me," Molly ordered. "I been working the garden. I thought you was someone else."

McCord seemed about to smile, then thought better of it.

The two men settled on the porch. Boone waited for McCord to open the case. "I'd be obliged for a drink of water," McCord said.

Boone disappeared into the house and reappeared a moment later. "Molly wants to know if you wouldn't as lief have ice tea."

"Water will do fine."

"Wouldn't be no trouble."

"Then I'll take ice tea."

Boone brought a tall glass, which McCord drank slowly. The violin case still rested across his knees. From time to time he polished it with his sleeve or flicked imaginary dust. It didn't help Boone's impatience to know that McCord was deliberately putting off opening the case.

McCord eventually set the glass beside his chair, wiped the corners of his mouth with thumb and forefinger, and smiled at Boone. "You be sure to thank your missus for me if I don't get to do it myself." He snapped the metal fasteners and started to open the case, then shut it. "The name Antonio Stradivarius mean anything to you?"

Boone nodded and smiled faintly.

McCord's eyes narrowed as he studied Boone to be sure he wasn't being mocked. "Of Cremona, Italy," he added as an afterthought.

"Are you saying you got—"

"I ain't saying what I got. First I have to be sure you know what I'm talking about."

Boone always figured if he lived long enough he would get to see a genuine Stradivarius in a museum or some place like that, but he never dreamed he would get the chance to see one up close, maybe even touch it or play a few notes. He leaned forward in his chair and rubbed his hands together to make them stop itching. He could feel himself begin to sweat. "Mister," he said, "if you got a Stradivarius in there I want to see it."

McCord lifted the cover and turned the case in his lap so that the gold-plush lining caught the sun. Then he lifted the violin, holding it with his fingertips under the body and the side of his other hand under the neck. Boone edged closer, excited by the soft texture of the varnish, then dazzled by the orange shading almost to red when McCord moved the violin slowly and let the sunlight slide over it like a warm wave. He dropped his eyes demurely, as though grateful to have found a man who could appreciate what he held but unwilling to take all the credit for himself. "Here," he offered. "Take it. I wager you ain't never seen nothing like it."

Boone backed off.

"Go ahead," McCord insisted. "It lasted this long, I reckon it'll survive awhile longer."

Boone reached for it but discovered his hands wouldn't move.

"I was the same way the first time I seen it," McCord smiled.

"A genuine Stradivarius?"

McCord turned the violin so that Boone could see the signature at the shoulder. "See that? A. Stradivari, Cremona, Italia."

Boone squinted to read the faint script and before he knew what he was doing McCord had popped the violin into Boone's hands and was unclipping a bow from the plush lining of the case. "It does my heart good to see a man who knows a beautiful fiddle when he sees one." He handed Boone the bow. "Go ahead, play something."

Boone shook his head. "Wouldn't dare."

"Hell, it's my fiddle. If'n I say you can play, you can play."

Boone tucked the violin beneath his chin, then immediately pulled it away.

"What's the matter?" McCord demanded.

"Better use a kerchief." He handed the violin to McCord. "Wouldn't want to sweat on it." Boone searched his pockets for something to put between his chin and the instrument. He pulled out a red and white patterned handkerchief and thrust it back in his pocket.

"What's the matter now?" McCord asked.

"It ain't clean."

"Clean enough."

Boone tucked the violin beneath his chin again. His fingers ran over the strings. Nothing in his life had ever felt so good to him. Not that he believed McCord one hundred percent. He touched the bow to the strings and waited for some avenging angel to strike him, because he didn't doubt McCord one hundred percent either. He pulled the bow boldly and waited again. "Needs tuning," he said and tried to hand the violin back to McCord.

"Then tune it," McCord said.

Boone clamped the violin between his chin and shoulder, picked and bowed the strings while he turned the pegs until he was satisfied. "You want me to play?"

"Unless you can think of something else to do with it."

"What do you want to hear?"

"Anything you want."

"I don't know any classical songs."

"Then play something else."

"How about 'The Orange Blossom Special'?"

"That'll be fine."

"On a Stradivarius?" Boone asked. If McCord wouldn't stop him, he was certain the ghost of A. Stradivari would.

"Why not?" McCord smiled. Then as if he could read Boone's mind, "The fiddle don't care what you play, and Mr. Stradivarius been dead for hundreds of years."

Boone started tentatively, but after a few bars, when he could hear how good it sounded, he got right into it. Molly came to the door of the kitchen to listen. McCord tapped his foot and clapped.

"I don't believe I ever heard it better," he said as soon as Boone finished. "How about playing 'The Tennessee Waltz' just to please an old boy a long way from home?"

Boone raised the violin again and played so sweetly there were tears in McCord's eyes before he finished. Then Molly wanted him to play "I'm Thinking Tonight of My Blue Eyes." And McCord wanted to hear "The Wabash Cannonball." Then he played "The Great Judgment Morning" and finished up with "Amazing Grace," with both Molly and McCord singing.

"That's about the most beautiful thing I ever heard," McCord said, and Molly agreed.

"It ain't me, it's this fiddle," Boone said and handed the instrument back to McCord, who put it in the case.

"Damned shame I got to sell it," McCord sighed, "but it ain't a question of what I want. And that's why I come to you." He paused to be sure he had Molly's attention too. "An instrument like this, well, it ain't the only one in the world, but there are damned few like it. Excuse my French, ma'am. What I mean is I wouldn't sell it without I had to, and I don't want just anyone who has the money to buy it. I want the person who gets it to know what he's paying for."

"How much you asking?"

"There's a sick baby back home and it's going to take fifteen hundred dollars to make her well."

Boone expected the price to be so much more that he almost said he'd take it before he could dicker.

"I know I'm talking big money," McCord said, "but both of us know that fiddle is worth every penny of it." He sighed again as though the thought of parting with the violin was too painful to contemplate for long. "What I need from you," he said, "is the name of someone who got that kind of money and who would appreciate what he's buying."

Boone pretended to consider the matter. McCord folded his arms over the case and waited.

"Can't think of a soul right off hand," Boone said. Molly started to name someone but Boone shot her a look and she shut her mouth.

McCord snapped the case shut and stood. "Well, friend, I thank you kindly. It don't do no harm to ask. And thank you, ma'am, for the ice tea." He reached down for the glass and handed it to Molly, who had changed into a striped cotton dress with a low neck that seemed to emphasize her bosom.

"Hold on, mister," Boone said. "You come this far you can wait another couple of minutes." McCord leaned against a porch pillar and brought the violin case to his chest so he could hug it with both arms.

"I could be interested in that fiddle myself," Boone said. He shot Molly another look so she wouldn't gasp. He knew she would never shame him in front of a stranger, but he also knew he would hear about it as soon as they were alone. "Fifteen hundred the best you can do?" he asked.

"If the doctor told me it would take fourteen hundred that's what I'd be asking. And if he said two thousand I'd be asking that. What's more I'd get it from anyone who knew a bargain.

God made just so much land and then he quit. There ain't going to be no more than what there is. Well, Mr. Stradivarius made just so many fiddles. What there is right now is all there's ever going to be. It stands to reason that if none of them ever get lost or broke they still got to get more and more valuable."

Boone turned to his wife and nodded. If she wasn't completely convinced, at least she wasn't gasping. "All right," he said. "Done." He stuck out his hand and McCord put the violin case in it.

"I can't give you the money until I go to the bank tomorrow to get a loan," Boone said and tried to return the violin to McCord.

"You keep it, friend. It's yours."

"Not until I pay you," Boone insisted.

"You don't strike me as the sort of man who would take advantage of a body," McCord answered.

They had a drink on it. Then Molly invited him to stay to supper. He declined but Molly wouldn't take no. After supper Boone asked McCord if he had a place to stay the night. McCord said he did. Boone didn't know where that would be, certainly not around Minks Mill, but to say anything would be the same as calling the man a liar.

McCord had barely left the yard before Molly began. "Just like that, fifteen hundred dollars and all you say is 'Done.'" She banged the supper dishes around the sink. She was always banging something when she was angry. "I swear if you ain't something else." She turned to face him, soapy hands at the sides of her stiff white apron. "It's not even like you don't already have a fiddle, two if you count the busted one that all it needs is a spot of glue to be as good as new."

There was no point in trying to interrupt her, not when she was like this. She would have her say. Boone filled his pipe and struck a match on the underside of the table.

Molly turned back to the sink and drowned her hands in the soapy water. "I don't believe a word of that story about a sick baby in Tennessee. It seems to me if you were bound and determined to buy his fiddle you could at least have dickered awhile.

I suppose I should be grateful he didn't say five thousand or maybe ten."

Boone tamped the pipe with the tip of his index finger. "Got nothing to do with the man," he said. "I don't believe he's even married, much less has a sick baby. It's the fiddle." He drew on the pipe, then tamped it again. "It just wouldn't do to dicker over a fiddle like that."

He set the pipe on the table and pushed back his chair. She could feel him come close, could have seen his reflection in the window above the sink if she hadn't kept her head down. When he put his arms around her she tried to squirm free. "Careful," she said. "I'm full of soap."

"And that ain't all." He held her closer.

She turned in his arms and rested her head against his chest. "I should have known never to marry a musician." She leaned back to examine his face. "There's more coffee," she sighed, "and I saved you a piece of pie."

The next morning McCord was at the house so early both Boone and Molly figured he must have slept in his car. Molly gave him a big breakfast, then the two men went to the bank in Beckton, Boone in his pickup and McCord following him in the blue De Soto.

McCord waited in the car while Boone conducted his business at the bank. There was no trouble about the loan even though Boone refused to tell old Mr. Austin what it was for. Everyone knew Boone was the best mechanic anywhere and a good worker when he felt like working, and there was the house for security. All Mr. Austin asked was that Boone agree to sign on with Sam Boatwright at the garage and work regular.

"That ain't so much to ask," Mr. Austin insisted. "It's only until the note's paid off. If you sit on your porch playing your fiddle and waiting for folks to come to you to get their cars fixed it will be forever before the bank gets its money."

Boone could see the logic of that and agreed, though it seemed ironic to be borrowing money to buy a Stradivarius and at the same time arranging so there would be less time to play it.

"How do you want the money?" Mr. Austin asked.

"Cash." Boone hadn't discussed the matter but knew without asking that McCord would want no truck with checks.

Mr. Austin didn't bat an eye. "I'll see if we have that much," was all he said.

Boone handed the bills to McCord and insisted he count them. "No need for that," McCord smiled.

"Count," Boone said, and McCord set the bills in piles of one hundred each, spread across the dashboard, then the seat.

"To the penny," he said and swept the bills together before stuffing them into his pockets.

The two men shook hands again, and McCord drove off while Boone walked across the street to Boatwright's garage.

It took close to five years of working regular hours to pay off the note, but the day Boone settled with Mr. Austin he packed his toolbox, put it in the back of his pickup, shook hands with Boatwright, and returned to being his own man, living off what Molly grew in the garden and whatever he earned fixing cars, when and if he felt like it. To make up for lost time he played the fiddle more than he ever had, at fairs and dances and funerals of course, but traveling any distance, and even playing at some places he was almost ashamed to take Molly.

He didn't tell anyone about the Stradivarius and made sure Molly didn't either. He had never been one to brag, and in some of the places he now agreed to play it wouldn't be good sense for people to know he owned anything it was worth their while stealing.

Boone remembered those years as the best time of his life. He could tell Molly felt good too. She was never more loving, and he never felt closer to her. His golden time, he called it during the bad times that followed. Like when he and his brother were boys and built a tree house in the oak beyond the barn. They lived in it all one summer, coming down only when they had to. As long as they were aloft nothing could touch them except the sun or the wind or the rain. They knew God held them in the palm of His hand, granting them a special providence not because they deserved it, but simply because it pleased Him to do so. Boone felt the same providence every time he picked up the violin. He didn't have to play it, just hold it in his hands and feel God's grace settle over him.

Then Molly got sick and the golden time was over. She had been feeling poorly for six months before she would admit something was wrong. Her weight kept dropping until she had no strength for anything. By the time she let Boone carry her to the doctor it was almost too late.

They operated on her at the hospital in Charlottesville and for a while she felt better. Boone had to go back to working for Boatwright to keep Molly in the hospital, but there was no way he could keep up with Molly's bill with what Boatwright paid, even after he was given a raise for promising to continue working regular. There was nothing for Boone to do but go back to Mr. Austin at the bank and take out another note. And even that wasn't enough. Those doctors at the hospital had to think he was made of money.

In the end there was just one thing left for him to do, but the very idea was so awful he put it off as long as he could. Each time he went to visit Molly all she asked him was what everything was costing and where would they get the money to pay. He told her not to worry but to concentrate on getting her strength back. The truth was he was worried enough for both of them.

"I know what you're thinking of doing," she told him, "and I don't want you to do it."

"No you don't," he said only because it was too painful to discuss.

Finally it became more painful to think about than do. After returning from visiting Molly he took the Stradivarius from its leatherette case for a last time and held it like you'd hold a nursing baby. Then he took out the bow, but he didn't have the heart to play. He packed up the violin and bow, set them on the seat in his pickup, and the next morning drove to Roanoke.

The first store he went to wasn't interested. The next one offered him fifty dollars. The last offered seventy-five. It was obvious that none of them would know a Stradivarius if they tripped over it. He didn't get mad at them and wasn't even disgusted. The only thing you could feel for that kind of ignorance was pity. What he should have done right off was go to Richmond, where at least there were folks who would know a Stradivarius when they saw one. On the way home from Roanoke he stopped to tell Boatwright he would need another day off.

The next morning he was on the road by sunup. It was a warm spring day, similar to the day McCord had appeared in his yard. He weighed what he could reasonably expect to get for the violin against what he would need for the bills. Ten thousand would show him a nice profit, he thought, though it troubled him to be thinking in terms of profit in connection with something he loved as much as that fiddle. Still some extra money would be nice, and there was maybe the chance he could find another. Lightning don't strike but once in the same place, yet it wouldn't hurt to be prepared. Five thousand was probably nearer what he could expect and Molly's bill would easily take all of that, so he didn't see how he could sell for any less.

He went to the biggest music store in the city, right on Broad Street, down from the railroad station, and asked to see the manager. While he waited he couldn't resist polishing the leatherette case with the sleeve of his jacket.

The manager was a short fellow with his hair long on one side and slicked across his head. He had a pale face with tiny broken veins and a neck that spread over his collar. Boone set the violin case on the glass-top counter and undid the clips. "I got to sell my fiddle," he said, "and I figured a big store like this would give me the best price." The manager picked up the violin and turned it over. "My wife's in the hospital," Boone added, "or I wouldn't part with it for any money."

The manager smiled and shook his head. "Hey, Bert," he yelled, "here's another one."

A tall man with stooped shoulders approached from across the store. He took the violin from the manager, held it up to the light so he could read the A. Stradivari signature, then handed it back.

"Where'd you get this thing?" the manager asked Boone.

"I bought it."

"From a man named McCord."

"How did you know that?"

"Every year we see maybe five or six genuine imitation Stradivariuses, and every one of them come from this McCord. Out of Kentucky."

"Tennessee," Boone said. He could feel the blood move to his face and the back of his neck begin to boil.

"You've been had, mister," the manager smiled. "But don't feel too bad. You're not the first and I dare say you won't be the last."

"I dare say," Boone echoed.

"The funny thing is it isn't a bad instrument," the manager said. "New it would probably retail for better than two hundred, but used I couldn't give you more than half that. Let's say one ten, including the bow and case."

Boone picked up the violin. "Thank you very much, sir."

"That's a more than fair price," the manger insisted.

"Yessir, I'm sure it is."

Boone walked stiffly from the store, imagining he heard the manager and his salesman laughing, and all the other salesmen and the customers pointing at him. He had meant to stop and see Molly on the way home and tell her she had nothing to worry about except getting well. Now he didn't see how he could ever face her.

At least no one else knew what a fool he was, no one except the people in the store and the other suckers McCord had taken, and none of them mattered. What mattered to Boone was that McCord had robbed him twice, first of his money and now his fiddle. The second theft seemed much greater than the first, but Boone was never the sort of man to take any theft lying down. He swore then and there if it took the rest of his life he would track down McCord. Jut thinking about what he would do when he caught up with the damned crook made Boone feel so much better he decided to stop and see Molly after all, though he wasn't up to telling her the whole story.

He arrived at the hospital fifteen minutes after Molly died. All the time driving from Richmond feeling sorry for himself she had been fighting to stay alive. The doctor told Boone he did all he could but they always said that. All Boone wanted to know was whether she went peacefully. Everybody said she had, but he suspected they were lying. It seemed to him the whole world was filled with nothing but liars.

And all the lies began with McCord. There was no dodging the issue. Boone felt the way he thought a priest must feel when he finally recognizes his vocation, or the way a knight from the Middle Ages felt as he set out on a Crusade to rescue Jerusalem from the Infidels. It was no longer a question of getting even with McCord or punishing him. And there was no court in the country would find Boone guilty.

Two days later he buried Molly in the New Providence Church cemetery. If folks thought it strange there was no music at the funeral, no one said anything. The bill from the hospital came to almost ten thousand dollars. Boone sold his and Molly's place—he had no use for it without her anyway—and had enough left after he paid the hospital to buy a scrubby place just outside town. He continued to work regular for Sam Boatwright to pay off the bank note, but every spare day he traveled to Tennessee. Of course he didn't expect to find McCord, looking for him on a part-time basis, but Boone couldn't stop himself from trying.

He kept his shotgun in the rack at the back window of his pickup and rigged a wire so he could hang the Stradivarius— he couldn't think of it any other way—from the rack too. In the glove box he kept a loaded .38 revolver. During that time if someone said something funny he might laugh, but he never smiled. He also started drinking pretty steady and putting on weight from having to eat his own cooking. As for the fiddle, he wouldn't touch it, wouldn't even listen to music.

It took better than two years to pay off the note, but the day he settled with Mr. Austin at the bank Boone quit Boatwright's, got in his truck, and took off for Tennessee. That would make it ten years from the time McCord first showed up.

The way Boone searched for McCord was to start in Knoxville, then work his way east by swinging north and south, bending back and forth until he was in the Smokies. Every place he came to, no matter how small, he asked around if anybody knew a Jesse McCord. Half a dozen times he found people who said they heard of McCord, some even thought they knew where he lived. Boone followed every lead but they all ended in cold trails. The more he failed the harder he looked. Sometimes he had to stop and work for a while to raise money. That was so much wasted time and he was back on the road as soon as possible.

For fourteen months Boone searched east Tennessee, always afraid McCord might have run to greener pastures, but knowing that sooner or later a rat goes back to his hole. Of course there was always the chance McCord would move in behind Boone, and that worried him some, but he knew he had all the time in the world because no matter how long it took, and how many times he had to double back, he would find the sonofabitch. Summer and winter Boone kept at it, and all the time he was traveling he never once touched the violin, just kept it hanging behind his head, under the shotgun.

Near the end of August he wound up in Pigeon Cove and was debating whether to go to Gatlinburg or turn west to Maryville. Something made him pick Maryville, and when he had looked there without finding anything he swung up the Little River Gorge to Walland, then to Kinzel Springs, Tuckaleechee Cove. In Townsend he found a woman who not only knew Jesse McCord but could say exactly how to get to his house.

It was late afternoon and hot. Boone knew he should wait until the next day, but having come so far and being so close, he couldn't stop. He followed the dirt road out of town, then swung left at an abandoned church onto a goat track, past a grove of silver poplars. All the landmarks were exactly the way the woman described them, but being so long away from Minks Mill he had forgotten how bad a road could get.

There was only one house, a run-down shack that looked like it was standing simply because it didn't know how to fall down. That had to be the house, but it was hard to picture someone like Jesse McCord living in such a place. An old man wearing a dark wool cap pulled low on his forehead and a tattered overcoat sat in a straight chair with his feet braced against the railing of the porch. He seemed to be asleep, but when Boone got down from the pickup he could see the man's eyes were open. He might as well have been asleep for all the life in those eyes.

"Is that you, McCord?" Boone asked.

The old man lifted his head but his eyes were still lifeless. He tried to stand, wavered for a moment, then sagged onto the porch rail.

Boone ran to catch him. It had to be Jesse McCord because Boone had followed the woman's directions exactly, and there wasn't but this one house, if that's what you could call it. He set the man back in the chair and looked at him.

Under what appeared to be a week's beard his skin was gray and dirty. The pencil-thin moustache had thickened and grew unevenly. His cheeks were so thin, his long chin made him look jabber-jawed. But it was his eyes, which had been bright and curious as a bird's, that were most changed. They seemed to have grown larger and become heavy. Maybe it was the way the skin sagged beneath them.

"You really Jesse McCord?" Boone asked softly.

"What's left of him." His voice was hoarse. When he turned to Boone, who bent over him, his breath was withering. "Who the hell are you?"

"Boone Eliot."

"Never heard of you."

"From Minks Mill."

"Never heard of it either."

"You sold me a fiddle," Boone said.

McCord sighed what could have been a laugh. "I sold hundreds of fiddles. You come to thank me?"

"I come to kill you."

"You're too late. I'm already dead. If I last the night it will be a damned miracle." He paused to catch his breath. "I ain't had a bite to eat for two days. No food in the house, no electricity, out of gas." He paused again, then laughed grimly. "And that's no lie." Tears filled his eyes and flowed down his sunken cheeks. He flicked at them with his tongue. "Had a woman to bring me food, but she took the car and I ain't seen her since."

"A redhead?" Boone said. "Kind of skinny with a big nose?"

"That's her."

"She told me where to find you."

"She would." McCord stood and grasped Boone's arm to keep from falling. "I done a lot of things in my time, but I swear I never done nothing to deserve to be like this. Please, mister."

He collapsed and Boone had to pick him up. He felt like a sack of kindling. Boone carried him into the house and tried to find a place to set him down.

There were no sheets on the bed and the mattress ticking was torn. It smelled of vomit and urine. Beside the bed was an orange-crate table and a kerosene lamp without a chimney. In the next room there was a table with three legs, an armchair with springs stuck through its worn upholstery, and an empty bookcase whose glass doors were cracked where they weren't missing. Beyond that was the kitchen with an antique gas stove layered with grease and a small sink hanging from the wall. Roaches wandered leisurely instead of scurrying through the mound of dishes crusted with bits of dried food.

From that point on everything Boone did followed in a kind of logic, though he fought it each step of the way. First he carried McCord back to the bedroom, pushed a torn blanket aside and placed him on the bed. "I'm going to get some food," he said. It was getting toward suppertime and there was nothing to eat in the house.

"It won't do any good," McCord groaned.

"I'm getting it for myself," Boone said. "Just don't die while I'm gone," he added, then wondered why he said it.

"I don't make no promise," McCord said and pulled the ratty blanket to his chin.

Boone unhooked the propane cylinder that stood outside the kitchen—it made no sense to have food and no way to cook it—threw it in the bed of the truck, and drove as fast as the road allowed, back to town. While the cylinder was being refilled, he bought bread, eggs, bacon, soup, some cans of hash, canned vegetables, and lots of soap. He also bought a new lamp and a gallon of kerosene.

When he got back McCord was asleep. From the odor it was obvious he had soiled himself. Boone looked at him for a moment, then turned and headed back to the truck, not even stopping to put down the sack of groceries. He had the truck turned around and was back on the dirt road before he slammed on the brakes and skidded. "Damnit," he shouted and banged his fist against the dash. He backed the truck into the yard and went into the house. "Should have known you wouldn't die," he yelled at McCord.

He stripped off McCord's clothes and washed him with the only cloth to be found. McCord complained of the cold and continued complaining while Boone looked for fresh clothing. There was nothing that wasn't torn, dirty, or already soiled, so Boone brought in his suitcase and dressed McCord in his spare shirt and pants. One step following another, and there didn't seem a way to turn back or even stop.

McCord still complained of the cold until Boone brought in the blanket he kept in the truck in case he got someplace that had nowhere for him to spend the night. Then he hooked up the propane cylinder. With gas on, there was hot water, so he attacked the mound of dirty dishes to have something to eat off. One thing following another. When he finished he checked on McCord. "Just wanted to be sure you didn't shit my pants," he said. "I'm going to fix some soup." The food was already bought and paid for, it might as well get eaten.

"It won't do no good," McCord croaked. "I'm the same as dead. You're wasting your time."

"I got it to waste."

Boone heated the soup, then brought it to McCord, whose hands shook so badly he slopped it onto the mattress and missed his mouth completely. Boone sat on the orange crate and fed him. What else could he do?

"You married?" McCord asked.

"Used to be. She died."

"Any messages? I'll be seeing her before you do."

"Not where you're going."

Boone fixed his own supper, did the dishes, then cleaned up enough so he wouldn't trip over things. He checked McCord to be sure he was all right. "You have to go to the bathroom you tell me." Then he went outside, sat on the porch and smoked a pipe. After a while he went to the truck and slept.

The next morning McCord was strong enough to sit up and feed himself, but his hand still shook so badly he had to lower his face to the soft-boiled eggs to get them in his mouth. Later he sat on the porch, still dressed in Boone's spare pants and shirt and his own overcoat.

Boone knew the only way he would get his clothes back before McCord died and took them with him to the grave was to wash those that were dirty. He filled a big pot with water, built a fire in the yard, and dumped the clothes in to boil.

McCord watched him silently, then finally said, "You ain't shaming me by doing all this."

"I know," Boone said.

"Why don't you kill me if that's what you mean to do? It won't take more than a push."

Boone didn't answer.

When he had hung the clothes to dry he pulled the filthy mattress from the house so the sun could get at it, because it made him gag every time he had to go near it, and he opened all the windows that would open. Then he sat on the porch steps and rested. "As soon as your clothes dry you can put them on and give me back mine. I guess I better wash them too as long as I got the pot boiling."

McCord pulled the wool cap from his head and mopped his face. What remained of his hair was still bushy but had gone white. "How long you been looking for me?" he asked.

"I don't remember. Long enough."

"And now you found me." He laughed and slapped the cap back on his head.

"You shouldn't have cheated me and told me that fiddle was a Stradivarius."

"I never did."

Boone snorted.

"You said what it was. All I did was agree with you."

"That ain't true," Boone said, "but even if it was you cheated me."

"Wrong again," McCord said. "All I done was charge too much."

"That's what I call cheating. What did you do with all the money?"

"Like the man says, most of it went for booze and broads. The rest I wasted."

Boone laughed. "I guess you're feeling better. Watch out, old man, you get too well and I might still kill you."

"I won't never get that well. You got the fiddle?"

"Of course I got it. It's in the pickup. Who would I sell it to? You shouldn't have cheated me the way you did."

"Maybe I shouldn't have." He paused and smiled. "But it was the only way I knew how."

"I really loved that fiddle," Boone sighed.

"The fiddle ain't changed," McCord said. "Why don't you get it and play me something?"

"Can't."

"Why not?"

"Just can't." But he was tempted. "Too much has happened. I lost Molly. I lost my money. And I lost the Stradivarius. I had to sell our place to pay the hospital bill. I had to go to work regular twice to pay off the bank. I been on the road looking for you for God knows how many months. And it all started when you drove into my yard and sold me that fiddle for ten times what it was worth."

"I ain't going to argue with you," McCord said. "Even if all that is true, it don't change the fiddle none."

"It ain't what you said it was."

"It never was." McCord took the cap from his head again and mopped his face. "That fiddle is just as much a Stradi-what-ever-the-hell-I-said-it-was as ever."

"Varius."

"I painted the name myself," McCord laughed. "It ain't wore off, has it?" Then he began to cough and had to hug his sides to keep his chest from exploding.

"You all right?" Boone asked.

"No," McCord managed to say. He coughed some more and his eyes filled with tears. "I better lie down."

Boone dragged the mattress back into the house, took fresh-washed sheets from the line and made up the bed. Then he helped McCord undress and put on a worn flannel nightshirt.

"See if you can find another blanket," McCord said. "I'm about to freeze to death."

"What do I care if you freeze?" Boone said. But he found another blanket.

While McCord slept Boone puttered around, cleaning the worn linoleum floors, nailing loose boards where he found them, to keep himself busy.

"Hold down the damned racket," McCord yelled when the noise woke him. "A man should be let to die in peace."

At noon McCord was too weak to get up and wasn't any better at suppertime. Boone carried food into the bedroom but all McCord could eat was soup, and all he wanted to talk about was where he should be buried. "Not in the cemetery in town. Don't no one know me there."

"That could be an advantage," Boone muttered.

"I want to be in the old cemetery behind the church at the end of the road. Some of my people are there."

"Don't you have family?" Boone asked.

"Nary one." His eyes, which were as dead as when Boone first came to the house, suddenly showed a trace of life. "Except you. See that I get a proper box and a decent funeral. I'd pay you for your trouble if I had the money."

"Maybe," Boone said. "But you ain't dead yet."

"You should have killed me when you had the chance. You would have been doing me a service."

"Maybe that's why I didn't," Boone said. He doubted Mc-Cord could hear anything he said.

"Tell Darlene she can keep the car and anything else she can find. The rest is yours if you want it."

"Who's Darlene?"

"That redheaded bitch who sent you out here."

That night McCord's coughing was so bad it kept Boone awake. Later it stormed with heavy thunder and sheets of lightning. Boone came in the house to get out of the wet but spent most of the night putting pots under where the roof leaked, then emptying them before they overflowed. Some time during the racket McCord stopped coughing and quietly died.

The next morning Boone had to carry McCord's body, wrapped in a sheet, to the funeral home because the undertaker refused to drive his new hearse over the rutted road to Mc-Cord's house. Then the undertaker had fifty reasons why he didn't want to use the old cemetery. He finally agreed when Boone said he would dig the hole himself. In for a penny, in for a pound, Boone figured, and a man ought to be buried where he chooses.

He half expected to see Darlene at the funeral and was disappointed when she didn't show. There was just the Baptist minister Boone had found, the undertaker and his assistant, and Boone, who unhooked his fiddle from where it hung beneath the shotgun, and brought it along.

It wasn't much of a service. Even if there had been anyone who knew McCord, there wouldn't have been anything good to say. As soon as the minister finished and closed his book, the undertaker and his assistant lowered McCord into the grave and left.

Boone shoveled the dirt back in the hole, then patted it into a smooth mound. It was hot work without a speck of shade anywhere. He dropped the shovel beside the grave, mopped his face with a checkered handkerchief, then sat on the grave to rest.

When he had caught his breath he took the fiddle from its leatherette case and tuned it. He tucked the handkerchief under his chin and raised the fiddle. First he played "Rock of Ages," "Nearer My God to Thee," and "Amazing Grace." Then because he thought McCord would have liked it, he played "The Tennessee Waltz" and "The Wabash Cannonball." For Molly he played "I'm Thinking Tonight of My Blue Eyes," which helped make up for his not having any music at her funeral.